PRETTY THINGS

VIRGINIE DESPENTES
TRANSLATED by EMMA RAMADAN

FEMINIST PRESS
AT THE CITY UNIVERSITY OF NEW YORK
NEW YORK CITY

Published in 2018 by the Feminist Press
at the City University of New York
The Graduate Center
365 Fifth Avenue, Suite 5406
New York, NY 10016

feministpress.org

First Feminist Press edition 2018

Les jolies choses by Virginie Despentes was originally published in France by
Éditions Grasset & Fasquelle in 1998.

This work received support from the French Ministry of Foreign Affairs and
the Cultural Services of the French Embassy in the United States through their
publishing assistance program.

This book was made possible thanks to a grant from New York State Council on
the Arts with the support of Governor Andrew M. Cuomo and the New York
State Legislature.

First printing August 2018

Cover illustration by Molly Crabapple
Cover and text design by Drew Stevens

Library of Congress Cataloging-in-Publication Data
Names: Despentes, Virginie, 1969- author. | Ramadan, Emma, translator.
Title: Pretty things / Virginie Despentes ; translated by Emma Ramadan.
Other titles: Jolies choses. English
Description: First Feminist Press edition. | New York : Feminist Press, 2018.
   | "Copyright (c) 1998 by Editions Grasset & Fasquelle"— ECIP galley. |
   Identifiers: LCCN 2017056600 (print) | LCCN 2018006832 (ebook) | ISBN
   9781936932269 (ebook) | ISBN 9781936932276 (trade pbk.)
Subjects: LCSH: Sisters—Fiction. | False personation—Fiction.
Classification: LCC PQ2664.E7895 (ebook) | LCC PQ2664.E7895 J6513 2018
   (print) | DDC 843/.914—dc23
LC record available at https://lccn.loc.gov/2017056600

To

My parents,
Dominique, the empress Caroline,
Hacène & Emil Louis-Stéphane,
Nora Hamdi Mehdi, Varouj, Rico,
Tofick Zingo de Lunch & Vartan

SPRING

CHÂTEAU ROUGE. A TERRACE, ON A SIDEWALK, IN the middle of construction. They're seated side by side. Claudine is blond, in a short pink dress that seems sensible but leaves some of her chest visible, the perfect doll, meticulously put together. Even her way of slouching, elbows on the table, legs spread out, has something refined about it. Nicolas's eyes are very blue, he always looks like he's laughing, about to do something mischievous.

He says, "Fuck it's nice out."

"Yeah, it hurts your eyes."

She forgot her sunglasses at home, she creases her forehead and adds, "I feel weird, seriously. Like right now, it's burning." She touches her throat and swallows.

Indulging her, Nicolas shrugs his shoulders slightly. "If you didn't pop antidepressants like they were candy, you'd probably feel better."

She breathes a long sigh, raises her eyebrows.

"I don't feel like you're being very supportive."

"Likewise. You could even say I feel more fucked now that I know you."

"I don't know what you're talking about."

He's tempted to get angry, point out that she isn't funny, but it stays lodged in his throat and he settles for smiling. The waiter arrives, flings down two coasters and two half-pints on top of them. Impeccable moves. The bubbles rise through the gold in straight, rapid lines. They clink glasses mechanically, exchanging a brief glance. At the next table, a kid makes noise slurping the bottom of his grenadine with a straw.

Nicolas stubs out his unfinished cigarette, really flattens it to make sure it goes out, and declares, "It'll never work. It's impossible to mix you two up."

"Good one, sweetheart, we're only twin sisters."

"So how do you explain that I didn't even recognize her when I went to get her at the train station?"

Claudine pouts comically, revealing she doesn't get it either.

Nicolas insists, "She passed right under my nose, I didn't raise an eyebrow when I saw her. It wasn't until all the passengers cleared out and we found ourselves alone, side by side, that I saw a vague resemblance between you and her."

"Maybe you're kind of an idiot. Have to take that into account."

The waiter passes by their table, Nicolas signals for him to bring two more of the same. Then, rubbing his forehead with two fingers, looks into the distance as if he were contemplating the issue. When he's had enough of not talking, he goes off again.

"She's nuts, your sister, totally insane."

"She's just grunge. Compared to the freaks Paris churns out, I find her pretty calm."

"There's no denying it. In the course of an afternoon, I heard her say exactly four words, and they were 'You can fuck off.' You call that calm?"

"Put yourself in her shoes, she's on the defensive."

"What bothers me is that you didn't even warn me. You forgot to tell me lots of things, I'm sure."

She tenses, turns her head toward him, and he knows this face, when she loses her composure and becomes downright nasty.

"Do you plan on being a pain in the ass all day? If it bothers you, then by all means, don't force yourself. Go home, don't worry about a thing. We'll make do without you."

She doesn't leave him time to respond, gets up and goes to the bathroom. The lock is all rusted and falling to pieces, yellow traces of cigarettes like scars on the toilet paper roll. Squat toilet, be careful not to spray your feet too much when you flush.

Chest struck with a strange heaviness, she wants to be somewhere else. Rid of herself. That horrible anxiety is ingrained, it wakes up at the same time as her and doesn't let up until she's had a few beers.

She sits back down next to Nicolas. A girl passes by in a combination of snakeskin and bizarre platform shoes. Farther off, a man yells, "Stop, thief!" Some people run and others get involved. Elsewhere, a honk, like a foghorn, as if an ocean liner were docking in the neighborhood.

Claudine rummages in her bag, takes out her cash and spreads it on the table, announcing, "No tips for assholes, that guy pisses me off."

"The waiter? What'd he do to you?"

"He doesn't even try. He sucks."

She pockets the pack of cigarettes and the lighter, concludes dryly, "So will you go with her or not?"

"I told you I'd do it, so I'll do it."

"Great. Let's go?"

She has a slightly satisfied glimmer in her eye. She gets up and waits for him, then in a relieved tone, "I love it when it starts to get hot out, don't you?"

Nicolas and Claudine have known each other for a while now.

The day she came to live in Paris. She remembers like it was yesterday. Decision made without any planning, she was talking to a girl on the phone, listed off their friends to bitch about them. She heard herself say, "Anyway, I'm taking off, I'm going to Paris, I don't want this life anymore, where tomorrow never means anything." And, hanging up, realized that she was really going to do it; they weren't empty words.

Filled a bag, this and that, whatever, the stuff people bring. Line at the ticket counter, first-class ticket even though she barely had a dime, for the symbolism; she wasn't going to arrive there like a fucking piece of trash. A little girl wouldn't leave her alone—"Por favor, madame, por favor"—Claudine looked at her, said no, but the little girl didn't let up, followed her all the way to the escalator. "Por favor . . . s'il vous plaît."

Spent the train ride in a strange mood, a budding impatience that would never leave her again. For real life to begin, whatever that meant.

Leaving the train station, she's struck by it all. The streets are enormous and packed with cars, commotion everywhere, all the Parisians hurried and stressed. She walked for hours, big eyes gazing out at the world, bag heavy and cumbersome, cutting into her palm and shoulder. At each street corner a new spectacle, imposing monuments and a flood of passersby. The smell of money was everywhere, an almost tangible current. And in her head, on a loop, *I will eat you, you giant city, I will swallow you whole.*

Night fell rapidly. Claudine all alone in a McDonald's, a guy came and sat next to her. Classy shoes, nice watch, all-around wealthy appearance. He made his preliminary moves, testing the ground, judged her favorable.

He was probably used to trying his luck with young women, brought her to eat at another place. A very chic restaurant, he must have deemed her worth the money.

When she said she didn't have anywhere to sleep, he felt he ought to warn her that he could only put her up for a night. Relieved all the same: it wouldn't be money wasted, she wouldn't take off at the last minute. Laughing, as if it were obvious, Claudine assured him, "I'm not going to move in!"

But she already knew that if she liked the apartment, she would stay as long as she wanted. She knew guys like him: male nymphos with a compulsive and insatiable need to be reassured, so vulnerable. She possessed everything necessary to control that kind of guy.

She played the girl who nearly cries because he made her come so good, then the girl who's grateful to be satisfied so well, just as quickly followed by the girl who doesn't get too attached, who isn't too curious or too talkative, discreet signs of admiration with a zest of *I'm used to people treating me like a princess so you better behave*, to nurture within him a constant latent panic and the feeling that he'd nabbed a real prize.

She must have done what she needed to because the next night the man insisted she move in. She resisted a little—"We hardly know each other, we're not kids anymore, living with someone isn't easy"—to make sure he didn't have any reservations. But right away he responded positively—"When love presents itself, you have to take the risk"—nimbly convinced that it inspired the same in her: a powerful jolt of rare passion. She certainly didn't deny it.

Life at his place was pleasant, even though he wanted to have sex all the time.

Disgust locked away, instinctively, that had always been her way, her exterior was all smiles, loving and serene. It stayed inside, her desire to vomit, and a certain astonishment each time: how incredible it was that people ever took anyone at face value.

Thankfully, most of the time he went out to do things, and she was left alone at his place. Let the days go by.

Paris was a more difficult city than she had imagined. Bursting with people just like her, set on carving out a good life for themselves. So she let time pass, worked out so that her body would be impeccable when the time came. Because the moment would come, she didn't doubt that yet.

A Sunday, winter sun, she went to the corner to buy some smokes. Long line of people at the only open tabac. A guy leaning against the bar was meticulously scratching his lottery ticket with a guitar pick. She watched him while she waited for her change. He was bland, sort of blond but not really, sort of tall but not really, blue eyes that could have been green, not poorly dressed but not well dressed either. Scraggly, nice smile, a nonchalance that suited him. Completely harmless, that was her first thought. Raising his head, he caught her eye, huge smile.

"A thousand bucks. I don't believe it! I never win anything."

"Maybe your luck is changing."

"I wouldn't go that far, but I'll take it. Can I buy you a beer?"

He was over the moon. A radiant sparkle somewhere in the blue of his eyes. He called over the clerk, winning ticket in his hand, showing it off, proud of himself. Turned toward her again, "So, are you having something?"

She had almost said no, purely out of habit of declining this kind of invitation. But she liked the look of his face, right off the bat. She thought it would be worth it to have a drink with him, accepted.

As for Nicolas, he examined this prized knockout, amazed to feel so entirely ready to trust her.

As far as bitches went, she blew everyone else away. Her white jeans and tight blouse like a second skin, accepting his invitation to have a drink. What did she want from him, with her big tits, her flat stomach, her curved hips, and why? She had a mesmerizing ass, and she knew exactly which pants to put it in.

They threw one back at the counter. She laughed easily, seemed happy to be there. He proposed, "Let's sit down for another?"

"Are you going to throw it all away on beer?"

"With all the debts I have to pay, it's already spent."

She had perfect white teeth. She played with her hair a lot, one of her ways of being ravishing.

"It's been ages since I had a drink at a bar. Not since I've been here, actually, almost three months. I don't have a dime, I can't even buy good cigarettes."

She waved her pack of smokes with an amused disgust. Then raised her beer to cheers him, waiting for him to clink his glass. She smelled good, he could smell her from his seat. She folded her hands on the table prudently, her nails were pink. It was impossible for Nicolas to figure out if she was dressed all trashy like *this is my thing*, or if she actually thought it looked good.

Later, after many more drinks, he asked her, "But why do you dress like such a slut?" Rolling her eyes she responded, "Listen, darling, you can feed me all the lies in the world, what I know is that all men adore this. Whether or not it's absurd is besides the point, what matters is that it works every time."

Three drinks later, she was telling him her life story: "I live with him, honestly he's nice. That's kind of the problem, I feel like I'm sleeping in honey. It's fine, it's sweet, but it's sticky, and besides, I've had better. Anyway, it's temporary, as soon as I find a way to make money I'll get a room, even a shitty one. Sometimes, when he's there, I go out for a walk, I look up at the apartments with balconies, huge windows, and yards in the middle of the city . . ."

And it was true, later on he'd see, when he was walking with her she would often stop, extend her arm to point out a window, "One day, I'll live there," and her eyes would light up, she was so sure of it, she knew how to be patient.

She kept talking, wasn't hard to listen to. "Starting out, it's like I'm expected to clean toilets without batting an eye. That's the only way I can be here, on the alert, but the first chance I get, I'll jump at it. It'll take the time it takes."

She chewed her bottom lip while she spoke, he noticed sometimes, asking himself if he was imagining the tears of rage that rose in her eyes.

She must not have been a regular drinker because she couldn't control herself at all, was in a daze, her eyes staring off into space.

"Why did you come to Paris?"

"To be an actress."

"In porn?"

It came out on its own, but you had to admit she looked the part. She just wrinkled her eyes, like she had swallowed something bitter. He stuttered, a vague hope of redeeming himself, "I really didn't say that to hurt you, I know a lot of girls who—"

"I don't give a shit about the girls you know, and I don't give a shit what you think of me. I'm not so naive that I don't know what I look like. And I'm not so naive to wait for someone to tell me what I'm capable or not capable of doing either. Time will tell where I end up. And I'll laugh at all those people who took me for an idiot. I'll show them."

She stood up straight as she spoke, her entire chest stuck out against the world, and then she slouched all at once, comically, self-consciously.

"But anyway, I'm also not so naive to think I'm the only girl to say that."

She kept quiet for a moment.

"Let's have one more?"

"Won't your man be worried?"

"Yeah. We were supposed to spend a wonderful afternoon together, watching dubbed action movies and smoking the disgusting pot he gets in the shitty part of town. The kids rip him off, I'm too scared to tell him. But honestly, we're smoking henna. Anyway, you're right, I have to get going."

"You want another or not?"

"Just a quick one."

The next morning, he got up to puke and she was on the sofa. He didn't really remember how she'd ended up in his living room. They had coffee, it was comfortable. She stayed with him until she found an apartment. They became friends almost inadvertently, by virtue of always being happy to see each other and always wanting to.

Three months ago, Nicolas—who was meeting someone near Claudine's place—went by to see if she was there. "Buy me a coffee?"

He found her overjoyed. "You know Duvon, the producer? He's down for the record, I have to call him as soon as the demo's ready. Listen, I think he's really into it. The guy really wants to give me a shot. I've been telling you about it for a while now, haven't I?"

He turned his eyes away from the TV screen where a guy—filmed from the ceiling for no apparent reason except to make it look shitty—approached another guy in the bathroom to shoot him in the head, calling him "my angel."

"The demo?"

"Yeah. I lied, I told him it was almost ready. I thought of your tracks, you know, the two I really like . . ."

"Not to throw a wrench in things but . . . Claudine, you can't sing, we've already tried."

Together they had tried anything and everything to get noticed. Wasted effort. Years piled up, ambitions dampened. More than anything else, what they learned was what to ask for from the social worker, what papers to falsify to get a certain kind of assistance, how not to get audited.

"I don't plan on singing."

Nicolas was flipping through the channels, stopped on a commercial where a completely crazy-looking girl illuminated by green lights was on her knees in front of a keyhole, eyeing a couple. An already-outdated image.

"Just tell me up front what you're planning to do, I'll never guess."

Behind him, Claudine put a cassette in the player and, before starting it, explained, "We'll send your stuff to my sister, and she'll plop her voice on top of the track . . . like she's taking a big shit."

"Your sister sings?"

"She's not bad. I'll play something for you."

"You have one of her songs?"

She rubbed the back of her neck like she did when something was bothering her.

"I sent her your stuff, that we had worked on, you and me, for her to give me a couple ideas. But she made her suggestions too complicated for me to replicate on purpose. I already told you how much of a bitch she is."

"You could have had me listen, so we—"

"No, she sings too well, it pisses me off. But I don't have a choice now."

She had chosen between tact and ambition a long time ago.

That was the fundamental difference between Claudine and the world. Like everyone else, she was calculated, egotistical, shit-talking, petty, jealous, a fraud, a liar. But unlike everyone else, she owned it—without cynicism, with a disarming nature that made her irreproachable. When someone criticized her, she would rub her neck. "Calm down, I'm not the Virgin Mary, I'm not a hero, I'm not a role model. I do what I can, at least that's something."

She pressed play.

After listening, he only asked, "Is it possible for her to change the lyrics?"

"No way. Nothing's possible with her, she's absolutely determined to be a pain in the ass."

"But she'll come here to finish production?"

"No way. She despises Paris. Which is for the best, because I despise her."

"You really look that much alike?"

"Don't you remember? I showed you a photo."

"But even now you—"

"We're twins, we look alike. It's not that complicated."

Nicolas admitted, "I really like her voice, we can make a lot of pretty things with it."

"Singing is the only thing she's good for. Lucky for her she knows how."

After that, as is often the case, nothing happened as expected.

"If you're not the one singing, what will you do?" Nicolas asked.

"I'll do the music videos, the interviews, the photos. I'll meet tons of people and then I'll start acting in movies."

"And your sister won't say anything?"

"No, Pauline can't stand anyone except for her boyfriend and two or three of her friends. I'd be shocked if she was angry about not being in the spotlight."

When the tape was done, Duvon thought it wasn't bad, just needed some modifications. Modifications made, there were still two, three things that he wanted to see changed. At this third stage he had shaken his head, very disappointed. "That's not it, that's not it at all . . ."

From that moment on, he became unreachable by telephone.

"Yet another thing going wrong," Claudine commented soberly.

But the tape made the rounds, some kid ended up calling her back.

"Well, some kid, he was definitely at least thirty, but he was in Bermuda shorts . . ."

One year later, she and Nicolas were walking along the quays, the leaves were starting to turn green, the girls were showing off legs they had already tanned, and a lot of people were out walking their dogs.

"He said, 'Come to my office,' so I showed up. I couldn't stop laughing, it was a totally disgusting closet with filthy junkies doing nothing but pressing buttons on the fax machine. And him, in Bermuda shorts. Pretty pleased with himself . . . I swear, it's too bad you didn't come, you'd have been cracking up. His label sucks, just shitty bands, his office is dirty, he dresses like a moron, but he's so fucking pleased with himself. As if he'd accomplished something. If the point of the game was to be a fuckup, then there'd be something to be proud of . . . birds of a feather flock together, you'll tell me, I'm sure."

"You think he'll make the record?"

"He says he will . . . he thought the lyrics were

'so cool.' I swear, I couldn't keep it together, the lyrics—what an idiot. Then he said to me, 'I'll do the record,' happy it won't cost him a lot, and he doesn't even know how to do promotion. Regardless, I signed the fucking dish towel he called a contract, we have nothing to lose, right?"

"You told your sister?"

"Yeah, yeah. She knows the guy's company, she knows all those shitty labels. She said it was cool, for once she didn't burst into tears. Maybe she's going to commit suicide."

"And she knows that you're saying you're the singer?"

"Yes, I told her. She's so sweet, she said, 'Go ahead, with all the talent you have, you have to appropriate wherever you can if you want anyone to pay attention to you.'"

"You're right, she's so generous."

"It'd be nice to think she's wrong . . ."

"Are you having a little bout of depression?"

"No, I don't give a shit. I've told you there's rarely a link between talent and success. I haven't lost hope."

"What if there's a concert?"

"There won't be. Maybe there'll be naked photos of me all over the place, but there won't be any concerts. For a start, if he manages to put out a CD, I'll be blown away. Want to go sit outside?"

Someone's playing the guitar downstairs. Deep chords stretched over a background of repetitive, sad sounds.

Claudine complains it's giving her an earache, she washes down her painkillers with Anjou Rosé. She's been drinking for a while. She walks around her apartment barefoot, soles black with dirt.

Sitting at a bit of a distance, magazine open on the

table, Pauline watches her, disgusted. Noise from the window, she glances over. Meat truck, a dumpster filled with pink and white. Some ladies are talking next to it, unidentifiable language, they're wearing elaborate dresses, summer colors, suddenly break into intense laughter that never ends.

Nicolas calls a friend, keeps flipping through the channels. On the screen, flashes of athletes dripping with sweat; zealous, pert, and abrasive female TV presenters; a prudent political man; a blond kid in a commercial.

Seated next to him, Claudine rips apart a cigarette. As soon as he hangs up, she asks, "So? Did he feed you a bunch of bullshit?"

"Less than usual. He seemed off. He was really disappointed you didn't want to talk to him."

"Absolutely nothing to say to him."

"In any case, you've certainly got him hooked."

"That's all they want, all of them. To collect women, it's the only thing that gets them off."

"You thought he was so smooth two weeks ago."

"I remember. But I must have some molecule, it's ridiculous, some thing that turns people into total losers. You take the coolest guy in the entire city, seductive, funny, open-minded, you leave him with me for one night and the next day he's dead weight. It's inevitable."

By now, he knows her little mean-girl schemes. Whether she sleeps with him or not, a man is still her worst enemy. The first time she lands a guy, she's as nice as a babysitter, all smiles between two blow jobs. Until the day she disappears. She pulls that move almost every time, to make them realize how attached they are. When she comes back, it turns serious, and the guys pay. Until the day it's no longer enough for Claudine: the gifts, the attention, the acts of love. Then, the final phase, she declares that not only is she seeing someone else, but she fucking loves it. Feigning sincere distress, she lets slip, "If you knew how hard he makes me come."

Nicolas takes a drag of the joint, coughs a little, remarks, "I'm glad we don't sleep together."

Claudine grabs the remote and looks for a channel with music videos.

"That would never happen, I'm not your type."

His type? He made a point of not fucking girls who think they're beautiful. Just to piss them off, those girls who think they have the irresistible gift of seduction. He figured out long ago that he's hot, that people really like him, without actually understanding why. He likes nothing more than getting a skank all heated up, until he can feel her really burning. Then not touching her. On the other hand, he has a weakness for homely physiques, the injustice of it gets to him, he really enjoys taking care of them, unearthing the good in them. At the very least he can be sure he's not the umpteenth guy to make them meow with his pelvic thrusts.

Claudine turns toward her sister, hands her the spliff.

"You still don't smoke?"

Pauline briefly signals no, her twin looks at the clock, adds, "It's almost time . . ."

Her sister doesn't even bother to respond. She continues reading, Nicolas turns his head toward her. It's still difficult for him to admit that this boring nerd, hair as lackluster as her skin, dressed in a sack, her gaze black when she wants something, really looks like Claudine.

Who says, "You okay, sis, not freaking out too much?"

"What the fuck do you care?"

"Wow, you're a real barrel of laughs."

"We can't all be a joke like you, Claudine."

Solid mastery of contempt. Nicolas stifles a snicker, elbows Claudine, convinced it'll make her laugh too, since she's normally so easygoing. But Claudine doesn't take the opportunity to laugh it off lightly. She usually makes fun of everything, or at least puts up a front, but she takes it badly this time, not even trying to hide it.

She swallows painfully, squints, spits out, "I guess we can't all be human either."

Her sister rolls her eyes, smirks slightly, snaps, "With how deranged you are, it's hard to feel any sympathy."

A few tears run down Claudine's cheeks, she doesn't even wipe them away, as if she doesn't feel them. Nicolas racks his brain, how to intervene tactfully and stop things from escalating. At a loss, he turns to Pauline, hoping she'll stop her bullshit. Pauline gets the hint, shrugs her shoulders. "She always was a crybaby."

Neither spoke another word to each other after that. Nicolas flips through the channels, pretending to be absorbed by a wildlife documentary. When it's time to go, Pauline gets up, stands in the entryway, waits for Nicolas. He looks her up and down, not wanting to believe it.

"You're planning to go out like that?"

"Yes. I do it every day."

"You have to put on your sister's clothes!"

"Don't count on it, asshole, I don't dress like a slut."

"No one's going to believe she'd go onstage like that!"

Nicolas, who saw Claudine often, had never seen her without makeup. Even when they slept in the same place, she made sure to get up first and get ready in the bathroom. Not to mention her obsession with clothes and the time she spent putting together the right outfits . . .

"Believe it or not, you can actually go onstage without dressing like a groupie."

"Have you heard of a little something called a happy medium?"

"That's for cowards."

He turns toward Claudine, counting on her support. She shrugs her shoulders in a sign of helplessness.

"Don't push it, there's no way. You shouldn't worry about it, there won't be anyone who knows me anyway, it'll be like I had a sudden grunge crisis. Could happen to anyone."

With a forced smile, without a shred of enjoyment. She accompanied them to the door, Nicolas lingered on the landing, still hoping for a word of goodbye that would ease the tension. Claudine barely looks at him, murmurs, "Don't worry, everything will be fine."

Monotone voice, closes the door, without the slightest sign of complicity.

Following Pauline down the stairs, he starts to detest her so badly he feels solidarity with those people who corner girls and force them to shit their little panties before using those same panties to suffocate them.

Rue Poulet smells like a butcher shop, whole creatures hanging from hooks. Women talking in front of packed displays of vegetables. On car hoods women sell underwear to other women, gesticulating, bursting into laugher, or throwing tantrums. A giant man lifts up a thong to get a better look, black lace stretched in the sun. Sidewalks strewn with crushed paper cups from KFC, food wrappers, green takeout boxes. Farther on, a guy sells pills in little plastic baggies.

It's not easy to get by with so many people on the sidewalk.

Accompanied by Nicolas, who's pouting because she didn't want to change, Pauline heads toward the metro. He shakes his head, pointing toward the taxi stand on the opposite sidewalk.

"I can't take the metro, I'm claustrophobic. We'll take a cab, it's not far."

She rolls her eyes, follows him without saying a word. His stupid struggle, the metro stresses him out. *I don't give a crap about your whiny bullshit.*

Her disdain evident since her arrival, her every look has been critical, condescending. She knows everything and judges instantly. How he would've liked plenty of disgusting things to happen to her, to break her in two and make her understand that everyone is doing what they can and that she isn't any better than anyone else. It's all relative. It's easy being perfect when you live under a rock.

He stares hard at her profile; they both have the same features. It only adds to his dislike. As if she'd stolen something from Claudine, something precious: her face.

There's always a truck at the street corner, either the cops or the Médecins du Monde.

At eight o'clock the doors of the Élysée Montmartre are still closed. The sound check is running late. A few bouncers are going up and down the stairs with worried looks.

At regular intervals the metro spits out people who

clump together on the sidewalk, filing into groups. Some people recognize and call to one another as if they'd just seen each other yesterday. No one thinks of complaining about the wait, unexpected and prolonged. Sometimes someone turns their head, deceived by a murmur in the crowd, gets up on tiptoe to see if it's moving, but it still isn't moving.

A woman carves out a path through the crowd, a kind of stubborn urban crawl. A bouncer listens to her sweet-talking—they're waiting for her inside for an interview—lets her flash her press pass. He pulls out his walkie-talkie to ask what he should do with her. He takes advantage of the wait to get a good look at her cleavage. Not because it actually pleases him, to look at her tits, he mainly just likes to make a show of it in front of his friends. As soon as she turns around, they'll have a good laugh about it.

The guy who works with him avoids meeting her gaze. Embarrassed for the man who skewers a woman like that, embarrassed for the woman who exposes herself like that. And embarrassed for himself because his eyes can't help themselves, they spring up and land on her. Every time he sees a woman like that—which is every time he works—he asks himself where it is she wants to go. He lets her pass, she climbs the stairs leading to the concert hall, pushes open the doors, and disappears. She scours the hall, looking for someone she knows.

She heads toward the food. Approaching the stage, she recognizes Claudine. *That bitch made herself look like a total dyke. Some people aren't disgusted by anything.*

The journalist scampers toward the stage, ecstatic at the idea of approaching her, of Claudine coming to shake her hand. Not that she would be happy to see her, they barely know each other, and the snob is hardly friendly.

Nicolas intercepts.

"Save your breath, she doesn't want to see anyone."

"She's getting a big head already?"

"No, but she's freaking out. Anyway, how are you doing?"

She could have smacked him. And that whore, up onstage, pretending not to see her and acting like someone who can sing. Whatever, it's not like they just filled the Zénith, she's only an opener. She acts like she isn't bothered.

"Listen, it's dumb, but I really wanted an interview. I can still talk to her after the sound check, right?"

"Not today, she's on edge, she doesn't want anyone to talk to her. You know, to really concentrate. But tomorrow, if you want, she'll give you a call."

"Tomorrow? That'll be too late. I'm afraid *I'll* be too on edge."

She turns on her heel and goes directly to the bar and orders a whiskey. Contemptuous anger: *What is this bullshit? Does she want us to talk about her or does she want to die in obscurity? She didn't even sell a thousand copies of her album and it's turned her into this.* But she knows very well that when creatives and journalists have common goals, plenty of things are forgotten.

Nicolas watches her walk away. For the moment, no one suspects a thing. Until now he's only experienced this level of absurdity in dreams.

Just then, the label manager worms his way to Claudine-Pauline. He congratulates her for a while. "Everyone's

crazy about the album, I'm so happy to have done it."
Standing nearby, Nicolas's heart comes out of his chest
and he imagines causing a diversion by throwing it on the
ground. But Pauline gets herself out of it, retorting, calm
and dry, "Shut your fat mouth, I don't want to listen to you
talk anymore."

Instead of being furious, Bermuda Shorts blushes,
starts stammering, perfectly cheerful. "Well then, she's got
some balls, huh, when she wants something . . ." in a very
administrative tone, which he never used while talking to
the real Claudine, who had always made an effort to be
friendly.

Nicolas walks across the entire venue, explains to the
sound guy for the third time that it doesn't make sense to
put the vocals so far up front.

Three hours ago, he couldn't have imagined that he
would make all these back-and-forths because the sub-
bass this or the equalizer that.

Pauline is onstage; hands crossed behind her back and
eyes glued to the floor, she begins to sing.

Stiff, not smiling, and dressed like garbage, she becomes
rather dignified. Quiet metamorphosis, impressive to see.
As though it were coming to her from afar, these things
pouring out of her mouth, so self-assured.

Nicolas climbs onstage. "Is the feedback okay?" He cautiously wraps the microphone in fabric. Then moves away
and asks her to sing again. "Can we try another song?" In
passing he argues with a guy from the venue who wants to
stop the sound check immediately because they're running
late.

He quickly adjusts one last thing, jacks tangled up
everywhere, the hall empty, stands exactly where he needs

to be to hear all the sounds, since he likes the sputtering from the walls, the knobs, the red lights, adjusting the mic stand, the guys hanging off the scaffolding to adjust a projector.

Like something you don't even dream about anymore, to avoid the taste of bitter awakening.

The guy from the venue turns plain nasty. They need to open the doors so the concert can begin.

Nicolas meets Pauline at the edge of the stage, notices her hands trembling. "I'm going to buy some smokes, I'm all out. You want to come with me?"

She shakes her head no, immediately reverts back to her usual demeanor; it makes him want to slap her. In any case, he's relieved when she refuses because he actually just wants to call Claudine from a quiet corner. Reassure her, tell her that everything's going well. And then a sort of guilt, this pleasure he gets from handling the sound check, as if colluding with the enemy.

"You want anything?"

"To be far away from these idiots."

Impossible to understand where her anger stems from. No one had spoken to her, no one had done anything to her. But it's not faked, she seems completely put off.

"Wait for me in the dressing room?"

"No, I'm going to shut myself in the bathroom. That way no one will talk to me. Come get me when you're back, I'll be in the one that's to the right when you come in."

"Everything okay, Pauline? A little stage fright?"

She stares at him hard, glacial. "Don't forget that we aren't friends."

That little surge of guilt he had felt from enjoying working with her disappears all at once. Crazy bitch.

THE THINGS IN her apartment are covered in a thin, viscous layer. Claudine washes her hands, the towel she uses to dry them seems greasy too. That happens, some days.

Sun, Xanax, enveloped in an almost absurd calm that makes her gently sweat, clammy torso and back. Her eyes close, are heavy underneath.

Nicolas just called: everything's going well. Not a surprise. Pauline has always been like that: successful at anything she sets her mind to. She can play the girl with a nasty attitude who's bored when she gets onstage. She knows her voice is good, she wants all the world to know. So she'll put on a good show, even if it's her very first.

Kitchen. Coffee rising, burbling up in spurts. The seal is busted, light brown bubbles leak out the sides. The coffee maker needs to be replaced, Claudine never thinks of it. Now that she has, she feels a slight pang in her heart because it no longer matters. Fear doesn't have much of an effect on her, just a small trace of bitterness.

She spills some coffee over the side, wipes it up with the sponge, which is slightly black from being poorly rinsed. She doesn't give a damn about household objects on principle: not to be like her mother.

Don't go, I'm begging you, don't go, there are things in life that you don't do, don't go . . .

Window open opposite, the street acts like a loud speaker, Claudine hears a song as if she were listening to it in her own apartment.

Sharp attacks tearing her apart, the same headaches of the last few days, but the banging is getting worse, less bearable.

Pink stain of the curtains, the sun setting. Irritated voices below. Reflexively, she leans out the window to see what's going on.

A man, back to the window in the butcher shop, two men and a woman facing him. It's the woman who's speaking, she's furious, hair covered, pink dress down to her ankles. The two men with her shake their heads to signal that they disapprove of what the third is doing. Impossible to know exactly what's going on, they're not speaking French. She can't see them well from so far away, but the man with his back against the security gate doesn't seem scared.

The flowers have started blooming in the last few days, hanging from other windows.

Her breath shortens, cuts off if she isn't careful.

How much longer are things going to be like this?

Luck doesn't change. It's all bullshit.

On a table, a photo of her and Pauline. They're nine years old, it's the only photo where they're together and dressed the same. It looks like a silly special effect, like a hidden mirror reflecting one face. Two queens on the same card.

She feels that terrible surge that passes through her from time to time. Anger, and she needs to retrace her steps to account for it.

Her father would repeat, "They certainly do look a bit alike, and yet they don't look alike at all," letting a knowing glance fall over Claudine. Supposedly he didn't talk about that in front of her, to avoid hurting her, supposedly he took precautions, because she couldn't do anything about it. She was the one who was not very clever, frankly, not very smart.

Sometimes her father invited friends to the house, called the two girls over. Secretive conversation, so they wouldn't hear, as if they didn't understand anything at all. Then he questioned them, to demonstrate to the audience how studious Pauline was: cunning, mischievous, and so sharp. And next to her, her sister, who never understood a thing. She did a bad job on her schoolwork, never connected anything with anything, couldn't convey the desired information. Filled with shame in front of these strangers, she had to open her mouth, say something, if she didn't say anything her father leaned in toward the other adults, said something mean, disparaging.

And her bitch of a mother, rather than defend her daughter, rather than put a stop to all of it, would bring her to bed immediately, infuriated at seeing her be so stupid. The next day, to console her, she would put her hand on Claudine's forehead, "It's not your fault, my angel. With twins there's always one that picks up the defects . . . my poor angel, there's nothing you can do."

Her mother's stomach wasn't big yet. She had just learned that she would be having two.

Her father was enraged. Since the beginning of the year her mother had been working, like him, as a teacher at a junior high school.

Before that everything had been clear, easily summed up: he had married an idiot, oafish and dull.

Of course, there were those weeks right after they met when her father would lean toward her—"You are my happiness"—and kiss her nonstop, craft compliments sweet as candy, talk dirty, he couldn't get enough of her.

And then slowly, as if he were opening his eyes, she became this meager thing. Inept. He didn't leave her, didn't cheat on her. He never got tired of watching her mess up every single thing she tried. Never got tired of watching her dress poorly, he who was so fond of elegance. Of hearing her speak poorly, he who so loved intellectual things. Every gesture she made was reproachable. Even her way of rinsing a sponge, of hanging up the telephone, of wearing a skirt.

He never got tired of watching her be so pathetic. And he pitied himself, to have fallen for such a woman. And without ever lifting a hand to her he went after her with all his violence, his entire being focused on demeaning her.

He wouldn't leave her alone until she cried. And as soon as her eyes watered, his fury would begin: How dare she complain? And what did she know of pain, the burning he felt?

The same way he demanded all the space in the bed, his own distress demanded all the space. He was the most, as a matter of principle. The most tortured, the most sensitive, the most in touch with his emotions, the most reasonable. The one of the two of them that counted, the one at the center.

She possessed only the right to listen to him because he loved to talk for hours. It was her duty to listen to him even if his words destroyed her, implied she was worthless, even if his words suffocated her, never left her any space.

And her mother let it happen, made herself sick, like a woman, in silence. Her body eaten up in big chunks that never completely disappeared, vomiting, careful not to make any noise, at night her ruined sleep knotted up her throat. But above all she would never complain, because he suffered so much. Compared to his experiences, hers were garbage, just showing off her melancholy, who did she think she was . . .

One day, she started teaching, like him, in the same junior high school. And in one year, everything switched.

Her mother turned out to be a good teacher, in any event perfectly capable of keeping the kids in check for the duration of class.

He had always been pretty mediocre, neither loved nor feared, interesting to no one, especially not to his students, who mocked his drinking; rather than picking up on the desperate beauty of the gesture, they picked up on his breath and used it to fuck with him.

And so one day, her mother, correcting homework, was interrupted by her father who, leaning over her shoulder, shared his opinion on a comment she had just written. Without even raising her head, frowning, concentrated, she replied, "Excuse me, but I think I know what I'm doing."

Her father's wrath was terrible. At first he tried to make her apologize, but since she persisted he started breaking things and insulting her like he never had before . . . the idea that she could even think of opposing him was intolerable, that she could draw the strength from somewhere to believe in herself in spite of him.

The rage of powerlessness, like a child's tantrum, took hold of him that night and for the first time he moved from threats to action, started breaking everything until she begged, fear in her eyes, until she was the first to give in.

Her mother quit teaching, shaken by having hurt him so considerably for a job that, in the end, didn't interest her all that much.

But her father stayed angry. He had always pulled out when he felt himself coming and ejaculated on her stomach, because he was too young to have a kid and because he wasn't sure—far from it—that he wanted to have one with her. From that day on, he started fucking her like he was nailing something into the ground, all the way inside so she would get a fat stomach and stay put.

But almost as soon as she was pregnant, her mother began to rise up and get comfortable with him. Supposedly she knew better than him about certain things regarding her condition. "Because I'm a woman," she would reply, shrugging her shoulders. Her mother proposed that they call the twins Colette and Claudine. Her father was firmly against it; she didn't concede.

"Then we'll each choose one name."

And so it was done, her stomach ripped in two.

THE VENUE IS filling up. Security regulates the flood of people, the bouncers glance in their bags, make them take off their jackets. It serves no purpose, to tell the truth, but it's part of the ritual.

At the top of the stairs people meet and chat, share rumors and opinions about what's going on. The stoner version of a social gathering, most of them are overly done-up: bleached pierced tattooed gap-toothed scarred high-heeled.

Nicolas moves through them, making himself look like he's in a hurry because he doesn't want to run into any old friends. It gets him so down, every time, makes him confront the reality of aging when he sees old faces again. Already a little wrecked, withered, fatigue settling in, and cynicism to top it all off, extinguishing what's left of their gaze.

Pauline, sitting fully dressed on the toilet seat, smokes cigarette after cigarette. She regrets being there. She's dreamed of this moment for a long time. But it was nothing like this. It was her own name, and Sébastien was there, backstage, proud of her as he heard her sing. And it wasn't in front of these idiot kids who've come to have their souls sodomized, ready to swallow any subversive commodity as long as it makes them think that it adds something to their identity.

Mainly, she misses Sébastien.

Chest strained by his absence, she remembers and lists the best things about him, like a little internal song playing on loop.

The first time she saw him she didn't really give a shit about him, he seemed like kind of an idiot.

Older than her, he had a car, drove her home.

Then there was that day: he brought her to her place and, sitting on the hood of his car, told her jokes. Claudine showed up, gave him her number. And when she walked away, Seb had remarked, "It's funny to see the two of you together. Your sister is super pretty. But she doesn't have what you have."

He was neither flustered nor aroused; he was the first boy to resist her sister's charms. To prefer her, Claudine's sister. So, in his arms, she realized that he was her entire world. And since then, nothing had ever weakened the hold he had on her.

Until one night in March, she had been waiting for him, irritated that he was late. They were supposed to go see a movie and he wasn't very excited, so she was getting annoyed looking at the time, convinced he was doing it on purpose. Then night fell and worry kicked in.

The telephone rings, the lawyer calling on his behalf. He was picked up that morning, in the papers they're calling it a "big catch," he'll have his sentencing soon, he doesn't know how much time Sébastien's facing, he can't answer any of her questions, it depends on who he does or doesn't give up. The lawyer has tact, a distant politeness, but doesn't care at all, just fulfilling an obligation: notifying the girlfriend of one of his clients.

Clean break, everything on hold.

FROM THE OTHER side of the door, some of the people working the bar are getting riled up talking among themselves.

"This crowd pisses me off, they're always trying so hard to be fashionable."

Another voice, from elsewhere. "When it's the Americans doing it, everyone thinks it's so *cute*, but when it's the French it's not funny anymore."

Aggressive tone, between people who have already been

drinking, trying to convince one another without seducing one another, sterile conversations that make up mosaics of meaning. Everyone is actually saying something different. An unhappy ex-child interjecting at every opportunity—sometimes while trying to affirm something, something else emerges—little pieces of poisoned cakes that we'd rather spit out.

Two girls loiter by the sink for a bit, she listens to them talk. They're probably washing their hands, touching up their makeup, redoing their hair. One of them says, "Two-hundred-thousand-franc advance, that's not nothing."

"But is the money for them or for gear?"

"It's for them, to get them to sign there instead of somewhere else. It's an advance against what the label thinks they'll sell."

"Two hundred thousand! Just like that, your problems start melting away."

"I'd certainly hope so . . ."

"For all the time you've spent slaving away, he must have no shame."

"That's definitely him: shameless. You'll never guess what he told me. He's going to give me two thousand a month—to pay the bills."

"No way."

"Oh yeah, he's a kid, this guy, he doesn't understand that he could pay the rent too. For him, money is pocket change, it's for buying his toys. I have to say, maybe I did let him take advantage of me."

"Still, with two hundred thousand, you'd have to be really stingy to only give away two."

They leave.

Then Nicolas's voice. "You in here?"

And as soon as she opens the door he tells her to wait five seconds. While he pisses he says, "It's nerves, makes me have to piss every five minutes. Does that happen to you?"

It's only right then that she puts a name to what she's feeling: panic and fear, like being up on the highest diving board. That emotion deep inside of her, anxiety mixed with a terrible desire to be elsewhere, to backpedal. And mixed with impatience, too, to feel its effect.

Pauline follows him backstage, asks, "Is it really possible for someone to give you a two-hundred-thousand-franc advance to make an album?"

"It's possible, but it doesn't happen to everyone."

"You'd need to already be famous?"

"Yeah. Or make everyone *really* like you."

SHE'S THREE STEPS from the stage, standing where there's no light. First rows of the audience, people gathered together standing and talking, red tips of cigarettes, general commotion. Two sound guys are moving around again onstage, taping up one last thing, moving the floor monitor a bit. She no longer feels her legs, nothing but her throat, it's like a chasm inside of her, she doesn't want to go onstage. Yet she's crippled with desire to be there, it makes her tremble through all her limbs.

Someone tells her she has to go on. She's in another time, no consciousness of anything, a moment when she does things automatically, hypnotized.

The stage plunged into darkness, the people below form a sort of flow of faces, a murmur runs through the crowd when she walks onstage.

She won't be able to do it. Or even move an inch, or even open her mouth. Spotlights on her, blinding, and the track begins. She has the time to think, *I'll forget the words and my voice will never come out.*

She's ashamed of being there and of everyone seeing her. She feels ridiculous, humiliated, exposed. And with absolutely no reason to be there, planted there, under the eyes of all these people. And where to put her arms and where to put her legs and how to disappear, not have to do this.

Nicolas looks at her, he's in the shadows at the bottom of the stage doing her sound mixing. He worries that something's going wrong but nothing's going wrong.

It's obvious that she's uneasy, awkward. The majority of the people in the audience don't even try to listen to her, they talk, wait for the real band. Some faces, in the first row, are attentive, heads moving a little. That's a start.

Even so, that voice of hers is so fucking rousing. It's not so much that it's well trained, but that she knows how to unleash it.

PAULINE AND NICOLAS go back home on foot. The sidewalks between Pigalle and Barbès show no signs of emptying, storefront lights, a mass of people. Some going to the prostitutes, others to have a drink, others to a concert, to the movies, to visit someone, to eat somewhere.

All kinds of people doing all kinds of things, like a big machine with everyone in their own track.

Nicolas drank quite a bit right after the concert, a backlash, the need to blow off steam. People around him, assailing him backstage, clamor of compliments, some sincere. Pauline was waiting for him, shut away in the can again. He claimed, "I don't know where she went," and so many people wanted to see her, puking up flattering words. Some insisted more than others, they really wanted to introduce her to so-and-so, playing the helpful middleman. He couldn't even leave, a crop of business cards and numbers scrawled on packs of smokes. Small success. Overwhelming.

He suggested to Pauline that they go back on foot, he needed the night air, still a bit cold, the boundary between the seasons. He talks to her on the way, mechanically.

She hasn't said a word since she walked offstage. Not one rude remark.

They turn down Boulevard Barbès, the street empties. To the right, the Goutte d'Or neighborhood like a chasm.

Fire truck sirens sound in the distance, get closer, turn into a racket.

Nicolas comments, "It sounds like they're headed somewhere nearby, maybe someone died. Last summer a guy got stabbed right below Claudine's window. They blocked the street, like in a Hollywood movie, and outlined the body in chalk on the ground. It was weird, you know . . . I was watching through the window, not the TV. They tinkered with two or three things, and then they removed the tape and in the blink of an eye people were on the street again. It was like life closing up over the dead guy."

There's a crowd at the end of rue Poulet.

"It's on this street!"

He walks faster, excited, but also concerned. "I hope it's not a dead body . . ."

Pauline listens to him blathering on, feels like he's trying too hard to act like a kid from the streets for it to sound believable.

They arrive at their destination, orange-and-white plastic tape stretched between them and the door.

Nicolas lifts his head, looks for Claudine at her window.

"Oh, she's not there. I'm surprised, with how nosy she is, this would be a jackpot for her . . ."

He signals to a guy in uniform, "Excuse me, we live here, can we go in?"

"Do you have ID?"

"No. We didn't realize we'd need ID to get back into our apartment. But there's someone waiting for us, who can—"

Pauline had pushed through the crowd, stopped at the tape. She turns toward Nicolas. "She won't be able to do anything at all."

He understands immediately, feels it in his stomach. One of the cops looks at Pauline, speculates delicately, "You're family? My condolences."

Stupidly, Nicolas reflects to himself that he really is the only one who doesn't find their resemblance striking. She hesitates, should respond with the truth but, coming from a concert where she was supposed to be her sister, doesn't know what to do. Her confusion passes for grief. The cop lifts the tape, signals for her to come through, announces, "She jumped. Some of the neighbors say they saw it happen."

A man asks her name, she says, "I'm Claudine Leusmaurt."

Nicolas flinches, a little belatedly, would like to intervene but she's already ahead of him.

"I'm the one who lives here. My sister arrived yesterday, we almost never see each other. It's a stupid thing to say but . . . I'm not all that surprised."

The man asking the questions scribbles some things in a notebook. He's doing what he's seen done in a lot of movies, adopting the gestures and mannerisms that seem appropriate for the occasion. Except it's obvious that he's bored shitless, thinking only of the forms he has to fill out. He snorts, asks, "She was alone up there?"

"Yes, I just got back from playing a show. She didn't like crowds, she didn't want to come."

She doesn't feel any emotion, except for something like hostility—*she always has to be a pain in the ass*—mixed with a joyous remorse. It's the third time she's wished for someone to die and it ended up happening: first her mother, then her father, finally Claudine. An empty space all around her, those who had to pay have settled their debts.

It's odd to see the living room completely filled with strangers busy with various things. Just like that, the room is transformed into a stage set, a normal place on pause, people fretting all around.

A man who must be a detective tries to get Nicolas to talk, but he's leaning against the window, doesn't say a word. Pauline is sitting in a chair, she intercedes, "He's really emotional, he must be in shock."

She gets up and takes him by the arm. "Go home."

She takes his hand, squeezes it to the point of crushing

it, and fixes her eyes on him. For the first time since her arrival, she plunges directly into him, he smells like metal. Her grip and her gaze, all authority. She asks, "Call me tomorrow?"

She waits for him to walk away.

Then, to the detective, "He didn't know her at all, she doesn't live in Paris. Get out of his hair and let him go."

"You can say she *didn't* live in Paris now."

"You're just chock-full of tact, aren't you, asshole."

He's set her off, a familiar feeling, she screams, "Son of a bitch, motherfucker, my sister just jumped out the window and you're saying shit like *that*? How fucked in the head do you have to be to act like such a dick?"

Finished screaming, a slight wavering. Those present seem tired, and must not like their colleague because they mostly take her side, understand where she's coming from.

They let Nicolas go.

She thinks over it all, the things she has to pay attention to in order not to contradict herself, not to betray herself. Now that she's become Claudine, she mustn't make a single mistake.

HE WENT BACK home to his 195 square feet. He sat down in the armchair that he reclines to sleep in. Put on his headphones and a CD. Still shocked.

He feels in him somewhere the stupefying banality of trauma. That efficiency cutting a life in two. A few seconds suffice to sum it up in one phrase: everything has collapsed.

He hasn't cried since he was little, he would really like to tonight. He doesn't know what it'll do for him, but like everything he's deprived of he lets himself form a splendid idea of it. He remains immobile, lets the ideas pass through him. They come and go, those flaying emotions, as they like. He doesn't have the energy to seek them out, nor to classify them, nor to shield himself from them.

He feels incredibly guilty. For not having guessed. The one time she let her true self be seen, he put off dealing with it for another day.

He feels it already, he knows he'll be angry with himself for a long time for having enjoyed this night so much. And when they walked back, he remembers clearly, somewhere in his mind he thought about how he should act, how to tell Claudine about the concert, thought of leaving out certain things to keep from hurting her.

But above all he regrets not having taken Claudine for a walk wherever, somewhere calm where she could escape her anxiety, switch it off. Reproaches himself for not being able to say, "Come on, we're getting on a train, we're getting out of here, I think you need a break."

There's a thought running through his head, repugnant and thoroughly misplaced, but a thought that comes back regularly, a nauseating regret: *Why didn't she leave me a note?* And: *Why didn't she wait for me, give me a chance to help?* Did he not matter at all, not have any impact on her life, not make any notable difference to her despair?

He had suspected something for weeks, behind the vestiges of agitation, something barely visible. He had noticed very clearly the pain intensifying inside her. He didn't have the courage to get involved. He thought it would ease up on its own, as often happens. The demon falls back into its slumber. He imagines a sort of bird, red and fiery, with a gold beak, ripping apart her chest, demanding that she surrender herself entirely to it that night.

Was it necessary, inscribed somewhere precisely what had to happen? Or was it nothing at all, all that was needed was a noise opposite, a phone call, a guy she likes on the TV, and the moment would have passed, would have been just like the others.

Did she have time to regret, the second after she had done it, to want to hang on, deny the evidence with all her strength and believe again in the possibility of survival? Did her life flash all at once before her, at the same time revealing and outlining who she was?

SHE SLEPT THE whole day, the noises outside mixing into her sleep. Woken up by an argument, she got up, groggy, glanced at the street. A man trying to hit a woman holding a kid in her arms, she insulted him while dodging his blows, ran away, the kid crying and extending his arms toward his father. Went back to sleep. The smell of the sheets made her vaguely nauseous. The sun struck her eyelids. The telephone in the next room rang and rang, tentacles of voices coming through the answering machine.

Then the day no longer filtered through the double curtains, she got up to eat something.

Muted and pure hostility, Claudine had always managed to piss off the world. Whatever scheme possible to attract attention. What happened that night was that she was so repulsed at not being the one under the spotlight that she preferred to go out the window. Sick with jealousy and always wanting to get herself noticed.

The whole night was tiring, a lot of strangers to deceive. In a trance, pretending she was Claudine, a sort of blind reflex. And she repeated to herself, "That cunt thought she was trapping me, but she's actually done me a huge favor."

Because that suited her just fine, to pass for her sister long enough to sign a record deal. That talk of an advance had been on her mind since she overheard it. She'll get an enormous advance and barricade herself in with the spoils. It came together little by little, a terrible confidence. Her sister knew people, Pauline would use her contacts and settle the deal in a month. Before Sébastien gets out, she'll have a fortune and they'll go off together far away from here.

But now she's alone like an asshole in this apartment. Alone for the very first time, with a heavy feeling, like she'd been drunk and done something really stupid.

Things left here, everywhere: open books next to the bed, pens, lipsticks, dirty glasses with alcohol hardened to the bottom, sweaters, a paper towel tube, coffee tin, empty packs of cigarettes . . .

In a corner of the living room, there's an entire wall of Marilyn Monroe. In every pose, at every age, from every angle, the Marilyns smile, lean toward the lens, want something, we don't know what, give the essential thing, a version of herself that doesn't exist. Just the day before, discovering this monstrous collection of clichés of the blond flaunting herself, Pauline felt mournfully indignant toward the childishness of her skank sister, who couldn't understand that what she was doing would only lead to disappointment.

Today, alone in the unfamiliar apartment, she thinks about tearing down all the photos, carving out some order in the pathetic chaos. But her sister is no longer there and it doesn't make any sense. Like many other ideas that come to her spontaneously, abruptly stripped of their logic.

Equilibrium needs to be restored. It was constructed opposite her sister, a force exerted on another. She has a clear image in her mind: two little women in a bubble, each pushing with her forehead against the other's. If one of the two little women is removed, the other immediately topples over, falls into the other's domain. A blank space, a void is created in her; in one night everything has shifted.

Noise outside, she stands at the window. The street lures her every ten minutes, the omnipresence of the outside. A kid runs, zigzagging through people, two cops run after him. Gendarmes and thieves. Passersby freeze, watching the action. Then the trio returns, going the opposite direction, handcuffs on wrists, flanked.

The day they arrested Sébastien, did they parade him around like that, in the middle of everyone, captured?

It's not just her at the window; all along the road, people lean out to observe and no one intervenes, no matter what.

To keep herself occupied, she puts on music and dances. She's always done that, danced just for herself. Sweat appears slowly, first on her shoulder, then her back, finally her thighs are moist; breath, heels, hips, and arms embody the music, all that she understands of it, she begins to sing at the same time, disorderly chorus, routine trance.

The telephone rings again, all the voices conveying the same badly feigned nonchalance. Her own cuts off.

"It's Nicolas. Pick up?"

She hurries to the telephone, picks up. "Hello?" with a strong echo because the answering machine is still on, she looks for the stop button, feedback. Pauline yells for him to call her back, hangs up hoping he heard her. The telephone rings again, it's him. He says, "So?"

"I was with them until six in the morning. Everything went well."

"What went well?"

"Becoming Claudine."

"What's gotten into you?"

"Reflex."

He says, plainly exasperated, "I don't know what to say."

"Can you come over?"

"What for?"

"We need to talk."

"I don't know what you're trying to do, but I know you shouldn't be doing it."

"Ring quickly four times so I know it's you?"

He agrees. As she suspected he would. As he will agree to all the rest. He's that kind of guy, always incapable of doing the right thing, attracted to bad choices and fascinated by chaos. She understands perfectly what he's like, what he can be used for.

She hangs up, looks at the things lying near the telephone: flyer for a special offer on delivery pizza, tube of aspirin, makeup artist's business card, journalist's business card, electric bill, an old *Pariscope* thoroughly underlined with blue and red—the things Claudine wanted to see—her

phone book, a number scrawled on an empty pack of cigarettes, and a planner plastered with Post-its.

All these things, a mess from another life. Pauline feels
an incredible contempt rising up in her; jumping out the
window really is a fitting end for a life lived in discord.
Weak bitch.

A videotape without a label, a validated train ticket for
Bordeaux, an art-house cinema's program, Pauline smiles.
*I really can't imagine you going to see Swedish films, you must
have had someone important to impress.* A little book that
cost ten bucks, keys to who knows where, a nearly empty
checkbook.

She pushes the video into the VCR, hits Play. Then she
takes the pack of cigarettes, dials the number, and asks for
Jacques. "Hi, hello, it's Claudine, I hope I'm not bothering
you?"

On the screen a music video is playing, really young
guys in suits, the famous Jacques is quite moved. "I didn't
think you would call me back. No, of course you're not
bothering me."

Claudine appears on the screen, quick close-ups of
her ass, she's not really dancing so much as grinding like
a half-wit, something that's supposed to be sensual but
there's nothing convincing about it. She looks more like a
crazy person. Terribly high heels, gold, with a strap around
each ankle.

"Are you all right, my dear?"

"Yeah, I'm great, just a little drained."

"Did you celebrate after your concert? You blew everyone away, I keep hearing people talk about it."

He has the voice of a young guy playing at being a

man. Like a protector, a cuddler. Pauline asks, "And you, your work, everything going well?" hoping that he'll talk about himself. She has to start somewhere. On the screen, Claudine has reappeared, same outfit, but she's on all fours, she moves her arms, probably trying to communicate *I'm a cat*. Pauline wonders if at some point she'll eat pâté out of a bowl.

The famous Jacques lists the many things he has to do, as well as TV reports for cable channels she's never heard of and a cinema dossier for a magazine that just came out.

She listens to him a bit distantly, makes little agreeable sounds, trying to get it through her skull that he's talking to a girl that he watches on all fours, and filmed from behind doing things like pretending to be a cat, whenever he wants.

He stops listing all the things he's working on. Pauline has a hard time understanding how anyone does so many things at the same time, and why a journalist as in demand as he must be—very, very important—is talking to Claudine like this. He asks, "And what about you, Jérôme told me there were a lot of important people at the concert. It seems they were all looking for you but you had disappeared."

"I was tired."

"Come on, you can't fool me. What kind of naughty business did you get up to?"

She doesn't respond. He doesn't take offense, he's all excited. "Just hearing your voice I'm hard. If you were here I'd shove it all the way up your pretty little ass."

"I'm not alone right now. I'll call you back."

Claudine is on the screen again. End of the song, she

throws a wink at the camera that's supposed to be mischievous. In reality, she looks like a fat cow that would rather be grazing.

Pauline sighs. Out loud, "Cunt through and through . . . and this you don't show me before asking me to pretend to be you. All those pigs that night thought they had seen my ass, and you didn't think to tell me."

She takes a blank piece of paper. Writes *Jacques* at the top, his phone number next to it, then writes, *Journalist for all kinds of media, knows a Jérôme, up to speed about the concert, slept with.*

The telephone rings again.

HE DOESN'T TAKE his eyes off Pauline. He must think that he'll impress her with his death stare. She doesn't react. He came to tell her that she has to abandon her plan, he had prepared an argument, but now he says nothing. That's his problem, she senses his weakness: he second-guesses too much, leaves an opportunity for his worst emotions to surface. And she knows what's holding him back in the first place. Because she suspects what will persuade him, she offers, "Coffee?"

And gets up to make it. He watches her, she has her back to him. She unscrews the top of the coffee maker, bangs the filter directly into the trash can to empty the old grounds, then rinses it under the water, cleaning it with her finger.

The same gestures. Which recall other mornings after all-nighters when he went there to have coffee, and the afternoons when he stopped by for a quick cup, and the starts of nights and the ends of meals. The countless times he saw her do just that. Familiar silhouette, he likes to watch it move. Intact shreds of a lost being, obsolete traces that he finds bewitching.

After that painful night, he only feels resigned. What was done doesn't provoke any conflict in him. It immerses him in an intense calm that he never knew before, distances him and pacifies him. A dignified sadness, without severity, he no longer feels anything but the sweetness of things, he reaps only memory's charms.

Her sister is crazy. As if she's carrying out a ritual whose secret only she knows. She communicates her request like it's a business transaction that would be unseemly to refuse.

"You have to listen to the messages on the answering machine. I'm not sure I completely understand, but I think they want us to make an album."

In this type of situation, he is always bewildered not to have someone on hand who he can ask to take care of the situation for him; he feels entirely incapable. Ditch her there. Call a doctor. Slap her silly, pummel her with his fists. He settles for keeping quiet. She insists.

"Listen to them. I need you to tell me what you think."

"Were you already sick in the head, or is it just the shock from yesterday?"

"I don't like your sense of humor. I'd even go so far as to call it shitty. If these people are prepared to pay for it, I want to make an album with them."

He holds his head in his hands, a funny gesture that he never does, mutters, "There's nothing wrong with that. You have the voice for it. But you don't have to be Claudine to do it."

"It'll make things easier."

"I don't see how."

"I want to get it done quickly. I don't want to meet twelve thousand people and introduce myself and be nice. Claudine knew tons of people, even if no one was interested in her they at least remember her legs. The telephone hasn't stopped ringing since yesterday, if we do it in her name, it'll go much faster. What I want is cash, and we have a way to get it."

"You're dreaming. You can't make an album just like that, you have to—"

"I'm not dreaming at all, listen to the answering machine."

Then, he realizes, "What did you say? *We* can make an album faster? You're counting on me for—"

"Everything. I don't want to see anyone. You do everything and you make the tracks. No offense, but it's probably the first time in a while that you've had the opportunity to do something."

"No way."

"Listen to the answering machine."

She plays the messages; at first he won't listen. She fascinates him a little, her reckless courage, she scares him a little too. Obscene stubbornness, she's a calm kind of crazy. And then the names catch his ear and he starts listening.

It's not the right moment, but he doesn't have time to stop it from getting his blood pumping. The number of calls, the eagerness of the offers. Incredible unanimity. During the concert, he wasn't aware of any of it. She blew their minds.

If Claudine had known that day. She was gone the night before. Exactly what she had been waiting for: the people with power ready to bid on her.

It's not a given that she would have taken it well. For two or three days, she would have called the long list of her enemies to taunt them deviously. Then she would have gone to see all those beautiful people who so wanted to meet her. Then she would have slept with everyone. Every guy, one by one, a clean and meticulous enterprise. She used to talk about that the way other people talk about alcoholism. The only way she had of avoiding it was avoiding men. "At least," she corrected herself, "not a man who I think wants me. If I catch a look, just one faint fraction of a look, it's like I smell blood and have to have the guy. I'm not talking about getting him in my bed, I'm talking about having him at my feet. And I can't stop myself."

Nicolas had been a survivor of the massacre. It was completely obvious from the first time they met, when he was with her he felt like he was with a little girl. Right away she had deemed him worthy of her trust.

All the messages had been played. He admits, "I'm impressed, you were a big hit."

Since the night before, he's felt broken in two, his heart flayed. He feels things really intensely, like he's under bright lights. He adds, "Listen, you put on a good show. Being mentally unsound never stopped anyone from singing well."

Pauline remains silent, seated next to him. He goes as far as encouraging her, advises her to call everyone back, and gets ready to leave. She persists, a phase of acute insanity. She looks at her knees, tenses her hands on each side of the chair, talks through her teeth, "I already told you I wouldn't go. If you don't do it for me, I'll go back home and that's that."

"That would be such a shame."

She interjects, "It would be like suicide."

"As you wish."

Outside, the garbage collectors go by, the racket of the truck and the garbage cans lifted tipped-over emptied.

Nicolas wants to end the conversation.

"I have no desire to stay here any longer."

She affords herself the luxury of a sardonic smile, insists, "Of course you do."

He smiles sadly, thinking she must really be losing it now. Except precisely at that moment he wonders what he's going to do when he leaves. Go where and see who to talk about what crucial thing. It's true, he wants to stay here. Between these walls, with this crazy woman, letting himself be fascinated by the scandalous resemblance.

She says, "I could really go for a whiskey."

He offers to go buy some.

On the way, he's still pretending to himself that he's going to reason with her. But in his gut he knows that he's going to go along with it. He has a soft spot for freaks, for certain people he can identify with, and he loves to curl up in their strangeness.

THERE ARE TWO windows side by side in Claudine's living room that look out onto rue Poulet. Nicolas and Pauline each take one, and leaning outside they talk irregularly.

They look down. A man passes, a bass guitar case in hand. A couple goes in the other direction, they're glued to each other, they don't talk and they slow down to kiss under the windows before taking off again. Apartment opposite, a guy types on his computer.

Pauline spins her glass of liquid fire, she has the feeling that everything has simplified. Her desires have become whole, less irksome, things are clearer, plainly outlined. And she finds herself laughing often. She forgets to ask herself how she's behaving, if what she's saying is right, she forgets to keep tabs on herself again and again and feels relieved. She asks, "Why did she do it?"

"I would feel less stupid if I knew. I was supposed to be her friend, the guy she could count on. And the only thing I noticed was that she took a lot of drugs . . . but I take so many drugs that I didn't even notice. I didn't find it strange, the desire to be wasted all the time, with the life we live."

"What kind of life did she live?"

"Didn't you ever talk on the phone?"

"She lied to me all the time. She's always been a compulsive liar, so I was skeptical . . . but I didn't think it would go this far. She said she would make some cash, a whole load of it. She said, 'In this city, money is everywhere, you can't even imagine. You just have to be in the right place at the right time and you've hit the jackpot—and I'm in, I'm swimming in cash.' I went through her stuff, there were bank statements. At first I was furious that she was on welfare because I thought it was some kind of scheme to get a little more while she was overflowing with money. And then I dug deeper, and she had almost no other money coming in . . ."

Nicolas doesn't say anything, lets her continue, taking advantage of her drunkenness to find some things out. She drinks more, a tiny sip, she's furious about what she's learned. She continues, "She told me she was a dancer, that she had so many things going on, she couldn't find the time to do it all. Modern dance. Since showing up here, I see why they call it *modern*. Same for the concert: she presented the idea to me as if it were pure generosity on her part, almost like she didn't need me. She knew everyone, the big shots in the area kept calling her, they were all crazy about her. There was a lot of money on the table, like I was lucky to get a piece of it. It could have been a reality, but she had no idea. Little Miss Liar."

"Everyone is like that here. Except for those who don't have to pretend to be important anymore because they actually are. This isn't a city where it's okay to fail. If you admit straight up that you're not making it, you make everyone else too scared, losers contaminate everything, like they're contagious—"

"It's the same for everyone. Why was it absolutely necessary for her to have a better life than the rest of us?"

"Because it's human nature. Doesn't that mean anything to you? *On veut vivre et pas survivre! Un deux un deux trois quatre.* We want to live, not just survive."

He moves away from the window and starts to do a sort of dance where he lifts one leg forward and then the other and hops in place, kicking the air. His head moves from right to left, he hums something at the same time.

Pauline watches and finds it bizarre to see him let himself go like that, it makes her think there's another him, barely still alive inside. Like a nesting doll, a new Nicolas enveloping another, but sometimes a younger Nicolas comes to take a victory lap and dance a little.

He's clearly very drunk. He's become quite red, already sweating a bit. He tacks on, "Do you know this one? *Quelle sacrée revanche! Je croyais là un mode de vie ce n'était qu'une vie à la mode!*"

He continues doing the same kind of dance, but with his feet together and moving his arms in a bizarre crawl, an unfamiliar jerk.

Pauline is embarrassed by it. She finds it funny, but she's embarrassed to see him lose control like this. He's showing her something that sober Nicolas wouldn't want her to see.

Pounding against the wall.

He stops abruptly, out of breath, yells, "I already told you never to pound on this wall again, you old bitch!"

But doesn't resume his wriggling. He looks for the lighter on the table, jostles the empty beer bottles, picks up a magazine, asks, "So you're that alone? There's no one from your old life that you'd regret never seeing again?"

"No."

She holds out the lighter that she had actually been holding in her hand, then pushes her glass toward him so that he'll refill it. She makes an effort to reflect, or to figure out how to explain it to him.

"Five minutes before I did it, if you had asked me, I would have said that I liked my life. And it wouldn't have been a lie. I liked my friends, I've known them forever, I liked my home . . . I've never really complained about anything. And then there was that reflex. I didn't have any other choice. It's so clear to me that there's no space for me to regret it."

"It's like that now, it's the shock of the news, but in ten days you'll be back to normal and you'll want to go home. Only you won't be able to anymore."

"What's done is done."

Nicolas tries hard to understand.

"Why do you hate her so much? Did your daddy love her more?"

He said it as a joke, except he hit the nail on the head. Pauline tenses, without even trying to conceal it, her eyes narrow slightly.

"She told you that?"

Claudine never talked about her parents. Until that night, Nicolas had never paid attention. She had never said a single word about them. He nods, "Yeah, she said it. She said that her father adored her, but that you had been a disappointment to him."

Then she starts to cry. Really huge tears fed by the eighty-proof alcohol. Even she is amazed to find it feels so good, after holding back so many tears and having so much weighing on her heart.

Nicolas watches her cry, without moving, without really knowing what he hit on, but the last drink was the clincher, the thing that glues you to the chair and entangles reason. He mumbles from time to time, "What I would give to be able to cry like that."

UNTIL THEY WERE ten years old, their father brought Pauline with him everywhere. Claudine hated her for that.

One day, it was school vacation, a room with bunk beds.

It must have been in the mountains, because in this memory they were in their winter clothes.

At the table, with friends, their father was running his mouth. An alcohol-soaked lunch, he had gone a bit harder than usual. His eyes riveted to little Claudine, ready to disappear under the table, he seemed on the verge of vomiting. "I can't believe you two came from the same stomach." Then he started to really heap it on, bringing his guests over to bear witness, who also would have liked to crawl under the table to escape his questions. "They look alike but one of them's ugly. Right? It's funny, there's barely a difference, it's just that bovine glimmer in her eyes, it makes you want to smack her. Right?"

The children were at the age when parents still speak bluntly, no matter what they're saying or how unbelievable it is.

Their friends took off earlier than planned, visibly angry. Their father had walked around in circles for a few minutes, gestured to Claudine. "Come here, you. You understand how ashamed you made me? Do you understand, you little cunt? Come here for your spanking, come closer."

And he had snapped his fingers like he was calling to a dog. The little girl approached, was given a good thrashing.

Behind her, her mother cried, "Stop it, don't work yourself up like that, it's nothing, stop . . ."

And as soon as he had walked away, she picked up Claudine, sighed, "You're always screwing things up, huh? Why can't you just make yourself invisible? Go to your room. Pauline, sweetheart, please go play with your sister. Make sure she doesn't make too much noise, so your father can calm himself down."

In their bedroom, Claudine was sitting opposite the window, swaying back and forth, humming something between her teeth.

Pauline hesitated for a while, searching for the words, then came up behind her, timidly caressing her hair. Mouth filled with tears, she had trouble expressing herself.

"You know, when he talks to you like that, it's like he's saying it to me."

She hadn't felt her sister's shoulders tense up. She continued, really starting to cry, "When he hits you I swear I feel it too."

Claudine stood up, turned to face her, grabbed her by the hair. Pauline didn't scream so that her parents wouldn't come. Claudine dragged her down onto the bed.

"You're sure you feel it?"

And covering her face with her hair, started to hit her, her little fists striking her face with as much force as possible. To really hurt her, she had taken the pillow and held it down against her sister's face with both hands. To be absolutely sure she was heard, she started to scream, "That's weird because when he kisses you, I feel nothing."

The door flew open. Her father came in, alerted by her screams. He wrested Claudine from her sister and threw her against the wall.

"I've had enough of you. You hear me? I've had enough."

Their mother had taken Pauline in her arms and was covering her with kisses, asking, "Are you okay?" One of them precious and the other tainted.

A few years later, insidiously, the order would reverse.

One summer, it might have been the very next, their father discovered he had a great talent for photography. In the space of a few weeks, Pauline had become annoying to lug around everywhere. The little girl's education had stopped interesting him. He had other things to do, important things. He came home before they were in bed less and less frequently.

Then, for a long time, he didn't come back at all. Without saying anything to the girls, he packed a bag, announced to their mother, "I need to isolate myself in order to create."

Pauline remained their mother's favorite. One birthday, when their father hadn't shown up, she came to tuck in Pauline, who slept in the same room as her sister.

"My poor baby, your father didn't think to call you for your birthday. He forgot you too . . . like your old mother."

Then she closed the door again without saying anything to Claudine. Double impact, nice shot.

In the dark Claudine gloated in a taunting voice, "The little baby whose daddy forgot her . . . oh he used to love his little girl. But now he loves someone else. Little baby, all alone."

Pauline lifted herself onto her elbow. "You shut up right now, we have to go to sleep."

"Did you know that the new woman he's with has a little girl who looks like you? But he says he likes her better."

"That's not true, he's not with a new woman. He left to work, he had to."

"It *is* true! Even you know it."

Pauline took it in stride, crossed her hands behind her neck, and assumed the tone used to tell fairy tales. "No, I don't know it. But what I do know is that Mommy, when we were little, she wanted to have an abortion. Back then, women did it with a coat hanger. The lady thrust the coat hanger into her and tried to pull out the baby, but I was holding on to you too tightly, so she couldn't. You were the one underneath, that's how you got coat hanger scratches on your head when you were still a baby. And that's how you got brain damage."

She could feel her sister shrinking into her bed, Claudine protested weakly, "That's not true."

"It is, Daddy's the one who told me but I never wanted to tell you because I didn't want to hurt your feelings. I waited until we were eleven years old."

Then Claudine started sobbing, couldn't get a hold of herself. Their mother came back, Pauline complained in a little sleepy voice, "Mama, I can't sleep, Claudine is pretending to cry on purpose to annoy me."

"Claudine, you'll stop your tantrum right now or I'll make you regret it."

And their mother closed the door. Then Pauline started taunting in her turn, "You think you're tough, but you're nothing but a crybaby."

It was during their father's absence that Pauline started to sing. Convinced that if she did something well enough for him, he would come back.

Every Wednesday, kids everywhere, an old lady taught them to sing *pomme pâte poire* while exaggerating their consonants, stretching their voices high and low and belting on pitch.

The old lady really liked Pauline, kept her after class. "You have to practice at home, don't forget. You have a very pretty voice, you have to practice every day, it's as important as your homework."

And the little girl didn't forget. She sang the best she

could, better and better, always vaguely convinced that this was how she would get her father back.

And he did come back. They hadn't seen him for three years. He squeezed their mother in his arms saying that she was the only one and that she had to forgive him. And for two whole months he was very loving.

He had this expression when he saw Pauline again, standing before him, embarrassed, ready to cry and bury herself in his arms, this funny expression: "How you've changed!" And a completely different expression when he saw Claudine again, making her spin around and admiring her from top to bottom: "How you've changed!"

One of them had become gloomy during her father's absence, refused to be flirtatious, found it degrading. Pauline had stooped a bit, shrunk into herself, became wary. She didn't like to wash her hair, she didn't like to wear skirts, she didn't like to smile. She really liked hitting others, insults and arguments. And she didn't much like girls, who she found too stereotypical: talking about clothes, cuddling, and whining over nothing.

Claudine, for her part, had seized on the fortune of having a body matching the fashions and really learned how to show it off, her adolescence more than making up for her few awkward years.

And so their father still preferred one over the other, but his target had changed.

Some mornings, over breakfast, when he saw Pauline arrive with her ripped jeans, her flat shoes, and her big sweaters meant to hide her entirely, he would sigh, "I wonder if she makes herself ugly on purpose, just to piss me off."

And since she would sit down without saying anything he would add, "Such a friendly little girl, it's a real pleasure living with you."

A few minutes later, Claudine would come down, wearing the shortest things, her eyes lightly made-up. Their father would give her a standing ovation, take her by the hand to plant a kiss on her cheek.

"How good you smell!"

Then he would look at her pensively, hands crossed under his chin, eyes staring a bit into space. Before starting to eat again, he would declare, "I love feminine women."

He never went to see Pauline sing no matter what. She was dumbfounded. Not that she fully understood it at the time, but all that she had learned from him and nurtured so skillfully under the assumption of his return—arrogance, anger, vindictive violence—he used against her when she tried her hand at them.

What I adored about him, he despised in me.

Reading these lines long after, things would fall into place on their own, a lyric would be the key.

All that she adored about him, he despised in her.

And she set out to sing even more beautifully, and wearing even larger sweaters because one day things would fall back into place. He would recognize her, his only daughter, his only double.

NICOLAS MUST HAVE been tired of watching her blubber; he went to lie down on the sofa and now he's sleeping. He breathes through his mouth, without snoring. All scraggly, like a dozing cat. So fragile. He will help her. She saw them together, him and Claudine, the connection between them was so strong it could have materialized, suddenly taken shape without surprising anyone. He will do everything he can for them to sign. Let's hope he can do enough for them to get a big advance.

She doesn't have a well-defined plan yet, but the two hundred thousand she heard mentioned before the concert keeps popping into her head. She doesn't want to go on TV, nor see herself in the papers, nor dance in a music video like she saw her sister doing. She wants him to heat things up, get a big fat check. Then she'll take off with Sébastien, without telling him, and he'll sort himself out.

She gets up abruptly, it came up without warning. Mouth full of vomit, she rushes to the toilet.

THE NEXT MORNING they guzzle aspirin and Coke.

"Even if I wanted to help, it's never going to work."

"Stop making this into such a big deal. Ever since I was little people have thought I was her, that doesn't just change overnight."

He sees in them all the same vague characteristics. They don't come out the same, but have the same source.

She goes to look for a notebook, then comes back to the telephone.

"Before you leave, can we listen to the messages together? You can brief me on each person."

She's already in place, ready to take notes, she adds, "There's some mail too . . ."

He sits down, ready to comply. Pauline has drawn three large columns: *work, personal, unknown.* She fills them in painstakingly, especially the work column. When they've finished she goes to look for the unopened letters, which she hands to Nicolas, then she writes something in her notebook. Very busy, taking charge of things, not panicking at all.

Despite what he had said at the beginning, it's eerie how closely they resembled each other.

And staying with her, taking part in her schemes, at least he's not losing everything in resuscitating Claudine. It's like when someone starts doing coke: convinced that he's in control, that it won't get out of hand. He does it under the pretext of lame excuses: *I'll let her think I'm going to do it, but I'll convince her to stop this charade, I'll reason with her.* He does it while managing to convince himself that he's not doing it.

Pauline conscientiously writes down what he tells her.

"That's a card from Julie. Claudine adores her but they don't see each other often. She's a girl with a kid, who's cool. I don't know her very well, she's pretty, really really pretty, and she's a stripper. I think she lives in the thirteenth arrondissement. I don't really know. That's a note from Laurent, an old friend of hers."

"I recognize the handwriting, I know him, it's okay."

"What are you going to do about the people you both know?"

"I'll act like I'm her, I'll laugh like an idiot as soon as someone opens their mouth, if they touch my ass I'll say, 'What do you think you're doing?' and as soon as any topic is introduced I'll pout a little and say, 'Oh that, I don't know anything about it.' You know, it's not rocket science to be a moron."

LIGHT OF MY life, my true love. It's a little cold, I feel it in my fingertips. I just made myself tea, I'm putting the bag in the ashtray, if you were here you'd grimace, "You can't put it in the trash?" I'm taking advantage of being all alone here to do the things that would bother you. The days without you here don't really feel like anything. But I'm not sure it would be too wise to complain. Otherwise I have nothing to report. I do nothing at all except wait for you, rest often, and read a lot. So things are fine. Please write me soon, tell me if you need anything, I'll write you more later.

Pauline

Nicolas says it's not possible to make an album in less than six months. Pauline says nothing, it doesn't change the fact that everything needs to be done by then. Or rather: it doesn't change the fact that they will need to have a big advance by then. She couldn't care less about the rest.

When Sébastien gets out, she's convinced herself, she'll have money, enough to travel around the world.

The visiting room. She doesn't go often. Sébastien told her in his letters, "Don't worry about it, don't come, write me every day, but don't come. It would do me a lot more harm than good."

And that's what she did. Stopped going. Stopped seeing him there for the allotted time and then leaving him behind. It drove her crazy each time. A useless rage of helplessness.

Don't even show how much it weighs on her, this lack of him, don't even show it, smile, be cheerful, and invent a little life for herself in which "things are fine."

She watches herself dress up, put on red lipstick, and train herself to walk, she watches herself attempting the impersonation. And she's half mad at him.

Where are you while I'm doing all this to myself? You should be here stopping me. He should have been there the day she said yes to Claudine for the concert. He should have been behind her to ask, "What are you doing?"

But it's bad to be angry at him, she's confusing everything. Blaming others for how we are.

Only it's not so bad, because everything will be fine. Nicolas will go to the meetings, and he'll come back with a big smile. Because everything will come together as it should.

PAULINE IS SITTING at the kitchen table.

She opened the shoe closet, nothing flat.

At twenty-five years old, she has never thought to put on high heels, and she finds herself grotesque in a red dress, like she's in drag, trying to walk in the living room with the lowest heels in the entire collection. Absurd attempt at a dignified walk that's even remotely passable. Ankle, in jeopardy, jerks to the side, knee knocks against the other knee. So she has to walk carefully, think: *Which do I put down first, the sole or the heel?* Think: *Where do I put the weight of my body so that I don't slouch? Hold myself upright, move the leg.* But it doesn't work, she looks like a drunk crab, nothing like a woman.

She looks at her feet, destroyed. Her heel is red from the abuse. Her toes are stunted, sensation of ground-up bones, because the toe of the shoe contracts and compresses with no regard to the form of a foot.

It will never work.

Her rage turns black. *Claudine, poor idiot, where did you get the idea to wear such things, who were you trying to make happy, to look like what, stupid pathetic slut.*

The telephone is ringing off the hook, ten times worse than yesterday.

"Claudie? Claudie, pick up I know you're there, I called five minutes ago and the line was busy. Come on, my dear, scamper over and pick up. Claudie, I have good news for you, come pick up . . . You're not there? Listen, I don't get it, call me back, it's Pierre."

She takes off the impossible shoes, immediate relief. In less than an hour she's gotten herself some magnificent blisters, transparent skin bubbling up from the rest.

Takes a bath, a little later. The vials, the bottles, the tubes, she puts everything in the bathwater, childhood memory of playing games with the toys floating around.

Eye pads, lotion, soft foaming cleanser, pulverizing exfoliator, mask of fruit acids and vitamin C or ceramide, things of every color, creams for nourishing this or that, silky skin, shiny hair, radiant complexion—relentless battle against yourself; whatever you do, don't be what you are.

Getting out of the water, she sniffs her arms, a mess of scents, all the things she had tried, an irritating odor, annoying because it's meant to be calming. Like how when we really badly want to fall asleep, fearing insomnia, we end up tossing and turning in the sheets fifty times, in a rage. A frenzy of serenity.

Red dress, her whole chest exposed, like a cow showing off her udders; the top of her ass, which no one should see, is visible. She spins around suspiciously in front of the mirror. A pang in her heart—she already doesn't look like herself.

Leafed through the pile of magazines that Claudine had been reading. Sheer panic. In a tone of amused complicity, a cornucopia of little tips for being a trendy slut. And getting into every single detail, making sure everything is in its right place: how you should orgasm and how you should break up and how you should shave and how you should dye your hair down to your pussy and how you should be, inside and out. A deceptively charming tone, idiotic propaganda dictating what we should be.

After centuries of having to completely cover themselves, women are now commanded to bear everything, to prove that everything about them conforms to society's expectations, to show they have recalibrated themselves: look at my endless legs, clean-shaven and tanned; my ass with just the right amount of muscle; my flat stomach and pierced belly button; my enormous, firm, and shapely breasts; my beautiful, healthy, ageless skin; my long eyelashes, my shiny hair.

Contrary to what she had believed, it isn't about submission to men's desires. It's an obedience to the advertisers, required of everyone. They determine the fad, page after page: here's what we're selling, so here's what you have to be.

"YOU SEE HOW well I'm managing?"

He agrees. "I do, and it must not be easy."

He watches her thrash about. She spins around, hops a bit, walks back and forth with some skidding, she can do a half-turn without her ankle buckling. She gets up on a chair, hands on her hips. She adds, "It's not perfect yet. There are some things I won't be able to do."

"Those aren't the right shoes for it."

Good progress, she was comical to watch at the beginning.

But she's been at it for a week, and now Pauline can manage in heels. Even though she has the same legs as Claudine and a similar walk, one thing clearly distinguishes them: how they present themselves.

Pauline gloats, "I'll be able to go outside soon!"

She hasn't gone out even once in the two weeks since she switched over. She says that it wouldn't be very smart, that you never know.

She's not exactly overflowing with common sense, another commonality between them. She has her little methods, extremely personal rituals that she has to follow to the letter "for it to work."

Nicolas remarks, "No denying it, they make your legs

look great . . . but maybe you should shave them. Or else get waxed."

"Are you crazy?"

He scratches his head, not convinced he'll be able to get his point across.

"You're really thinking of going out like that? In a dress, in heels, and your legs not done?"

"My legs are done, my mother put me in the world with them. It's barbaric, shaving, completely barbaric."

As if he had just proposed that she shave her pussy and show it to the whole world. A blatantly indecent proposition. In the past two weeks he's grown used to her bizarre reactions.

She strikes him as a babe in the woods. For years she's lived behind closed doors with nobody but her boyfriend, who seems to be extremely weird. She has never cheated on him, she has never thought about it, she doesn't have close friends, no one to miss, she doesn't have TV because it propagates too much bullshit, doesn't read magazines for the same good reason. Being that sheltered, she has her odd reactions.

He thinks it over, she certainly won't learn from the books she reads that women never show their body hair. Nevertheless, he attempts a demonstration.

"Still, you've gone into town in the summer, right? At Bar-le-Duc, there are people outside?"

She acquiesces. Fairly stubborn, for her the issue is resolved: she's already done enough of this, she doesn't want to hear talk of painful finishing touches. Nicolas continues, "Have you ever seen a single girl with hairy legs in a dress?"

"I don't look at girls' legs."

"That thug you're dating never asked you to wax?"

"No. He's not a thug, maybe that's why."

Why does he fundamentally believe that just because she's a girl she has to rely on artifice or else no one will want her? With all her heart, she wishes Sébastien were there so he could see what it's like, when you're different.

Nicolas goes rifling through the cabinets, takes out sugar and water. He's in a good mood, her reluctance really seems to amuse him. He proposes, cheerfully, as if they were about to play a game, "Come here, I can do it with sugar. I did it to my sisters when I was a kid."

"I said no."

"Listen, I, personally, don't give a shit. But since you really seem to want to make people believe you're her, I'm here to help, that's all. Otherwise, you can't wear a dress."

"No, I want to wear a dress."

She never wore dresses. Except at home, her big T-shirts. Otherwise, she never went out with bare legs. The usual drill: be as far as possible from Claudine, opposite, different.

And when she went out with Sébastien and they passed a girl showing off her legs, he always found it shameful that women always feel obligated to parade themselves about, exhibit themselves in order to please. He'd say, "Your purpose isn't solely to conform. It's like they're complicit. I don't understand them."

Now she's doing exactly what she shouldn't do, just to see, that's all. She absolutely wants to go out in a dress.

And again: her legs, in front of the mirror, ankles strained by the heels, calves, straight up to the top of her thighs . . . she has the same legs as her sister. Which are the same as those of women in the fashionable films they saw when they were kids.

She absolutely wants to go out in a dress. And since Nicolas insists, she lets him prepare his odd mixture.

It's the first time he's contributed to the plan without her having to push him. He's loosening up, slowly. Becoming more agreeable.

HER HEELS CLACK against the parquet, making little nicks in the wood. She starts to get used to it, she's ready to go out, just has to find the keys. Pauline goes from one room to another, not bothered at first but getting annoyed now, looking in corners, lifting up magazines, moving the clothes she had piled up after trying them on, throwing them in a ball, searching them again, she can't find the keys. It's almost absurd, she turns around in circles in the dump and then starts to overheat.

She is dressed completely in pink, a skirt that goes down to her knees, a rarity in Claudine's wardrobe. Her hair pulled back, hours in front of the mirror trying to keep it from frizzing out in every direction. Stubbornly, she doesn't adapt, she doesn't look like she's supposed to. Even when everything is done well, something about her acts up. In the bedroom there were small boxes, red stones, blue, amber like water or a funny mauve, gold or silver metal to wear around your neck, fingers, wrists, ears, and even fake things to wear in your nose. In a drawer, elsewhere, neatly arranged in little boxes, other spoils: makeup, colors for lips, eyelashes, eyelids, or cheeks, different textures, a painter's palette, all impossible to apply herself. Nicolas, leaning over her for several days, turning her head, absorbed in what he was doing, manipulated her face, looking for the light, explaining that she couldn't put too much on because she doesn't know that about herself yet, which colors do what to her, and goes flipping through magazines, confident gestures, to teach himself how it's done. Manipulation as an art form. And then her own face, vaguely changed, distancing itself from her. She quickly understood that he wanted, more religiously than he realized, more actively than passively, for her to slide more toward Claudine. She was surprised to see him searching for her with so much care, trying to break down her methods, what she did to make her eyes look so much bigger, to make her skin seem as soft as the skin of a fruit. He had very gently shown her. Pauline frowned. "How do you know how to use a makeup brush?" He responded, "My entire childhood, I watched my sisters do it," and fussed around her.

Today, she is finally ready to go out.

She is supposed to meet Nico somewhere other than Claudine's. She even has to take the metro, cross a large part of the city. As it turns out, the keys are hanging from a nail. Nicolas probably hung them there without thinking about it, having always seen Claudine do it.

On the staircase, it's not as easy to wear heels as it was in the apartment. The floor's not the same, this one seems more slippery, and it's not the same ankle exercise, going down the stairs. Clinging to the rail, Pauline, cautiously, step by step, arrives at the bottom. Kitchen smells mixed with odors of wax, noises behind certain doors. On the ground floor, the super pulls his curtain aside an inch, Pauline nods at him.

She presses the wrong button on her way out; intending to open the door she turns on the light. Then finds herself outside. She imagined that after days shut inside it would take a few minutes to get used to it, but it wasn't a big deal.

Except that the street she had been watching for a while from the window is different now that she's on it. Opposite her, on the sidewalk, two very tall and excessively large women; the orange one pushes her as she walks by, deliberately, shoves her with a powerful jab of the elbow. Then goes on her way. Pauline takes a few steps to the side, slips off the sidewalk and leans on a car. Nicolas had advised her once, all charm, "You just have to think of it like skating—there are a few tricks to learn and then it'll be fine."

Difficult to move forward on the sidewalk. Too many people, some block the front of the grocery stores, their baskets full of improbable things, others talk right in the middle of everyone, others seem sapped of all energy.

She walks with her eyes fixed on the ground. She passes a guy and her eyes look up at him instantly, identify him. He's the first white guy she's seen since turning down this street. Strange reflection to make. She is so not used to these shoes that for the first time she notices the difference in consistency between one place in the sidewalk and another. She also realizes that no one on the street is looking at her, as if she were transparent. The woman from earlier who'd jostled her, as if resolved to pass right through her, had signaled, *You aren't even here.*

Glance in a shop, beauty products, wigs. She passes in

front of a hairdresser, then a butcher's shop, then arrives at the metro.

The boulevard she has to take is on a slant. In normal shoes she wouldn't have noticed, it only slopes downhill a tiny bit. In high heels, the difference in level is insane, a truly perilous exercise. She sets her feet down one after the other, concentrating as though she were on a balance beam, trying not to fall flat on her face in front of everybody.

People watch her. Some even turn around. And others permit themselves close-ups with impunity, her legs, her ass, her tits, her mouth, some smile at her, or make little noises and whistles to entice her. She wishes she could pluck them all away; she can only move forward in small measured steps and act as if she hasn't noticed anything.

A man on the sidewalk is selling corn from a cart, the smell of grilled food, he calls to her, a sort of kind enthusiasm, as if wanting to play with a dog. A woman veiled from top to bottom is waiting for her ear of corn, she scrutinizes her, only her eyes visible, inspecting her, scorn tinged with anger. The seller keeps at it, even when Pauline is several yards past him, he continues making a big racket. She is entirely public, approachable, entirely made so that everyone pays attention to her. She's dressed for that.

Glance in the window of a jeweler's, full of gold and clocks. Her own appearance. Between fright and amusement. She looks like other girls, not herself. She never thought it was possible to go out like that without someone shouting, "Where's the costume party?" Her appearance, legs on display, silhouette transformed. And no one realizes that she's not at all like that. For the first time she understands: in fact, no girl is like that.

She's arrived at the bottom of the boulevard, her shoes already hurting her ankles, she waits to cross, a crowd of people. A hand slides along her lower back. Contact all the more obscene because it's slow, heavy petting, not furtive, a hand lingering on her ass. She turns around, impossible to know who did what, he's laughing isn't he, and in any case what would she say to him? Pauline feels like she might collapse at any second. It's not only the shoes but also the skirt, which is too tight. The light turns green, she follows the crowd toward the other sidewalk. Glances around, the entire neighborhoods stinks of poverty, like being in another city, another era too. And at the same time like something alive, howling with laughter, uninhibited.

Metro stop Barbès, the pigeons coo and shit on the columns, two guys selling melons, a lot of people, next to her a woman sings softly in a lovely deep voice, a man hands out marabout cards, the ground is littered with them: pink, green, blue, yellow.

She takes an open passage but realizes you don't pay here, you go directly into the metro without passing through the turnstiles. Pauline passes two young girls with their still-growing boobs and their formfitting pants, towering shoes with square heels and tops revealing their stomachs. When she passes they call her a slut. She stops, turns around to face them, they notice and slow down, one of the two is nervous. "What do you want from me, cum dumpster? What do you think you're looking at?" Already people are slowing down around the three girls talking to each other loudly; when there's a chance they might hit each other or . . . people gather right away.

A guy selling vegetables shouts to them, smiling, "Easy, kiddos, easy," and comments to his colleague, "When they beat each other up they're like the Furies," grinning like he'd really like to see that.

The girl insulting her has something gruff about her, she's bawdy and brutal. It's funny, jewels on her wrists, eye shadow on her eyes, princess clothes, and a way of moving and talking that makes her look like a boxer. Immediately she yells that she won't allow her, the dirty slut, to talk to her like that. Nailed to the spot, Pauline stammers, "We can't talk to each other like this, us women." It makes the girl burst into laughter. "Dirty whore, who do you think you are?" Her friend drags her by the sleeve. "Let it go, you can see she's crazy. Come on, let's get out of here, we're going to be late." A little circle forms around them, still no one intervenes, it's a lazy attention. The nastier one's cell phone rings in her purse, she takes a moment to look at Pauline and spit in her eye, "Us women . . . stupid dyke."

And walks away. Pauline finds herself alone again, right away a man approaches, a comforting gentleman, graying temples, he's a little taller than her, he puts his hand on her forearm. "You shouldn't stay here, mademoiselle, come . . ." and he pulls her away, she leans on his arm to climb the staircase, her ankles are hurting. He says, "With how ravishing you are, you shouldn't be in this neighborhood, that could have been dangerous, you know. You're not from around here, are you?"

As if it were perfectly natural for there to be neighborhoods she shouldn't be in. He asks where she's going, follows her to the platform. He's happy to be next to her, holds her close, he says, "I'll accompany you to your destination, it'll spare you from any more unpleasant encounters." As if it were totally natural for her to need someone with her.

Pauline shakes her head no, asks him to leave, she says, "I just want to be alone."

"You don't understand," the guy starts to insist, to give her compliments, as if she just had to be flattered, compliments on her clothing, "It's rare, these days, a woman who aims to please men," as if it were a shame that that was the case, as if it were owed.

She looks straight ahead of her, refuses to look at him too much. Did the mother of this old, very gallant gentleman dote on him to such an extent that he now believed all women exist to be nice to him, looking simply to "please" him? Does he find it pleasing that she's dressed like a whore, should she be flattered? She repeats that she wants to be alone, she gets more and more disagreeable, he doesn't take it badly, instead he's amused, as if she were a child. She pushes him away violently—"Let go of me right now"—and all chivalry stops, through clenched teeth, without backing away: "Don't come crying back to me if you get raped in a back alley, you hear me?" She repeats that he needs to back away, he's suffocating her, this old man, with his kindness that only wants one thing, to screw her with his mangled and disgusting dick, and she has a responsibility to be friendly, he still won't leave, his eyes have changed, now he's saying things he doesn't even mean: "What are you doing in the Goutte d'Or, huh? I've seen you girls from around here, you like to get fucked by black guys, huh?" And she shoves him with both hands, forgets her heels and her skirt, once again people are staring, he's not discouraged, he says to her in a low voice, "You don't want to see mine? If you like getting fucked by guys with big cocks, you'll be satisfied, you'll see. Is that it, huh, you like big black cocks?"

Then a younger man with a ponytail intervenes, his jaw animal-like but he's well dressed, all inflated with authority, he asks Pauline, "Is this man bothering you?" She wants to be able to tell him, *Mind your own damn business*, but the other man scares her so she nods yes. The younger guy chases off the old guy like a mangy dog, and the old guy, who it seemed nothing would drive away, immediately takes off, like a thief.

Pauline doesn't thank him, Zorro is very happy to play the hero in this situation, he asks her, "Are you okay?" full of menacing benevolence, all gentle, "You're sure, you're okay?" He rolls his eyes. "I'm ashamed to be a man, sometimes, ashamed of how we act."

She thinks, *I'm ashamed to be me, incapable of scaring him off, ashamed that he wouldn't even listen to me and you show up and it's over*. She stammers, "I'm fine, it's okay . . ."

The guy stays next to her, he has taken the place of the other guy, he'll look after her until it's safe.

They get in the metro car, another girl who saw everything says, "She's the kind of whore who looks for trouble, she's not satisfied until guys fight over her."

The guy smiles. "She's jealous," leans toward her, "you're extremely pretty."

First she feels anger toward Claudine: how could she reduce herself to being treated like this, flaunting herself and risking—

Then her anger shifts: Why can't she just be left in peace?

The guy is saying, "You don't look like you're doing so well, would you like to get out and have a coffee? You're so pale."

And she responds calmly, "I would like for you to

go to hell, asshole. That would give me back some color."

He gets up and leaves her, final looks exchanged, he seems sincerely hurt, not his pride, but hurt as if he's ashamed. She immediately regrets having hurt someone who might actually have been cool, in the end.

She looks around her, a guy gives her a big smile. Other people are plunged in their books, a kid waves hello to the people on the platform opposite, his mother asks him to sit down.

Glance at her watch, she's been out less than fifteen minutes. This plan is off to a really great start.

A LONG AND narrow bar, in reds. Containers of straws, mustard and ketchup like in America. The waitress is extremely pretty, all wrapped up in black jeans. Long fragile legs and something bright and vulnerable about her, like Bambi escaped from the big screen.

Nicolas looks up at her, she smiles at him sweetly. Girls all say he has the eyes of an angel. *Some guys have all the luck*, he thinks with satisfaction.

Next to him, three young girls, eyes lined in black, talking around a cell phone. One of them advises the other, "Go on, teach him a lesson." The other goes one further, "You have to scare him a little sometimes or he won't respect you." Then they start searching for who they could call that would know what was going on that night. They're wearing T-shirts that are much too small, modern bras that make their tits look almost aggressive.

Pauline enters, one of the girls looks her up and down briefly and pointedly, then leans over to whisper something, and the others turn around before bursting into laughter.

The twin sits, pulls her skirt down to hide as much leg as possible. Then sighs, abandons the idea, and lets herself sink into the bottom of her chair, arms dangling, mouth open. "This is the last time I go out dressed like this."

Nicolas takes the bun off his hamburger, removes the pickles, and adds a dollop of mustard. She admits, "Okay, I spoke too soon, I take it back: it's not so easy to act like a moron."

"Seems to me you're managing just fine."

"Until now, when I saw girls all dolled up, I imagined it was impractical and took a lot of work, but this much of a hassle, I had no idea."

"That's part of what forces you to respect them, that they inflict so much pain on themselves."

"Forced respect, huh? I mean fuck, when you go for a walk in this city, it's an adventure every fifty feet. No one ignores you. It's even more annoying because it doesn't add up: you can't tell me that other girls, because they wear a skirt, are gangbanged twelve times a day. I don't get it."

"You should've taken a taxi."

"Well that's obvious. I just won't go out anymore, that's one solution. What a life. I'm finished. This is the first and last time I mess around with this stuff. Tomorrow, I'm going to buy myself normal shoes and take the metro without anyone pissing me off."

"You said you want an advance, right?"

"Exactly."

"Then you'll stay dressed as you are. And you'll come with me to see them."

"That's enough, I'm not a whore."

"No, but if you play the part of a woman convincingly, they'll double their offers."

"That's bullshit. They liked it the other night without me needing to—"

He raises his hand, a sign that there's no need for her to continue.

"You're right, it doesn't matter at all. It doesn't have an effect on anyone. Totally, no one gave a fuck about Claudine. Those guys who called to see her, they just want to know her thoughts on Heidegger or the evolution of grunge . . ."

The waitress arrives, her pad in hand, Pauline opens the menu while signaling that no, she doesn't know what she wants to eat yet, the girl turns around right away. She has a stubborn air, small visible forehead, hair shiny and in place. Nicolas watches how her ass shakes as she scrubs the table.

"What are you doing looking at girls like that? Shit, it's degrading."

"To have a nice ass?"

"To be looked at like a piece of meat, like she's in a window."

She doesn't have time to elaborate, a voice suddenly shoots up behind her, "Claudiiine!"

Recognizing someone, Nicolas pales. Keeps his cool, whispers in a low voice as the guy arrives, "The time has come to see if you can pull it off . . ."

A hand grabs her neck, a warm palm insists on the embrace. Lips that kiss her not very far from her own, mouth that lingers a bit, making the most of her skin.

She waits for it to be over, for him to straighten up so she can see what he looks like. A disgusting mug, almost pitiful it's so ugly. His eyes are too small, like those of a dim-witted animal. He lets a hand hang off her shoulder, extends the other to Nicolas. "Philippe, Mémémusic."

Nicolas shakes his hand. "Nicolas. I produce stuff for Claudine."

He detaches his first name from the rest of the phrase, as if putting it in quotation marks. Pauline wonders what's gotten into them, appending their work to their names so spontaneously.

Philippe slides his hand down her back, a clammy and possessive caress, a show of familiarity. She reflects for a second, then asks him, "We're close friends then, you and me?"

He chuckles. As if she had just tickled him. She takes his wrist and removes it roughly. "You'll stop touching me if you want us to stay pals."

He wrings his hands, flashes a little embarrassed smile, falters a bit, "This is new . . ."

He throws a glance for help at Nicolas, who's now absorbed in the menu, two fingers on his forehead, very concentrated. The big idiot standing there is disarmed, like a kid whose mother just smacked him and he doesn't understand why. So he stays there next to the table, thinking of something to say to resolve everything, but coming up short.

Pauline ends up offering, "It's time for you to leave."

"But what did I do?"

He no longer tries to put up a front, to pretend to be the kind of guy who brushes things off. His face shattered, he's sweating from forehead to chin, the vulnerable wounded man. That makes her angry, she shakes her head, gestures to Nicolas, and reprimands, "It didn't even occur to you that he might be my boyfriend, and that I don't want someone to paw at me like I'm some whore right under his nose?"

"But I didn't—"

"You've gone and fucked everything up. Are you happy?" Genuinely furious.

Nicolas clears his throat, isn't sure whether to burst into laughter. Waits for the guy to leave, his back as stooped as his chest had been puffed up when he arrived. Nicolas says, "He must have really liked her. He looked completely destroyed."

"Yeah, right. I'm sure it must upset him to no longer be able to jerk off like a hog between her tits. Did you see how he was staring at my chest?"

He admits, "Pretty successful for a first impersonation, but it would be better to show some tact from time to time. It's important not to insult the whole world. Also, I'd appreciate it if you could manage to sort yourself out without involving me in your lies. I don't especially care to get my ass kicked."

But actually, he was fairly pleased by it, the way she gestured to him while asserting roughly, "Hands off my man's property." It was stupidly comfortable to assume the role.

Not far from them, a guy seated on a stool is staring at her intently, his sights also set on her cleavage. Pauline feels him and squirms, surly.

In a depraved, but also kind of friendly way, Nicolas is excited, to see her subjected like this to all their gazes and wanting so badly to escape. As sexy as she was stubborn, it gave her a pretty vibrant charm.

He changes the subject.

"You weren't scared?"

"I'm used to it. All my childhood, I had the chance to play this game. Almost every week someone would stop me in the street thinking I was her. She didn't tell anyone she had a twin. So people couldn't have suspected that the same person was actually someone else."

Nearby, the three girls are reading their horoscopes, letting out big screams that turn into fits of laughter. They laugh as if putting on a show, to prove that they are there and can do as they like.

Then Pauline asks the only question that truly interests her. "So, did you see the people from the record labels?"

"Three meetings yesterday, two today. My cell phone has been ringing nonstop . . . man, I'm good, it's insane how good I am."

"So?"

"They're going crazy. They all want us to sign. I said, 'Okay boys, but we can't sign everywhere . . . So what's your offer?'"

This makes her laugh. She can tell he really likes it. He's ready to launch into a detailed explanation of what he saw and what they said. She cuts off his momentum, "So how much?"

"It's not that simple."

"They gave you an amount, didn't they?"

"Stop acting like an animal, it's like you haven't eaten in two months. Why does the idea of the advance get you so worked up? That's not the only thing that matters."

"For me, it's only about the advance. I want to know how much these bastards are willing to blow when they get all riled up."

"A lot. It's driving them crazy to compete for the same thing. Everyone wants you at any price. I think we can get around a hundred thousand."

"All at once?"

"It's not a guarantee, okay? It's doable, eventually, if we're lucky, if they stay this excited—and especially if you decide to come with me."

"Not right away."

"You have to come, they have to get hard, and I'm not the one who'll do that for them."

"You could make a bit of an effort, you know."

He turns to one of his favorite topics: how they'll spend the advance. What equipment, what studio, what sound engineer, what saxophonist. Every time they see each other he talks about it for hours, as if he were constructing a house and didn't want to make a mistake in the plans. As if he had been waiting for this for a long time.

She nods her head now and then, asks some questions: "What does an extender do?" "And who else has he played with?"

Even she's surprised that it's already happened; she feels neither shame nor compassion. Without any hostility at all, she's going to throw everything away. This album that he clings to so much. She has absolutely no intention of recording it. She dreams only of the advance and of hiding away somewhere to wait for Sébastien.

Nicolas can go on repeating, "One hundred thousand sounds enormous, it is, but for the music industry it's not even . . ." He makes her laugh. She's already picturing herself on the beach, Sébastien there with her.

SUMMER

HEAT, AND NO MATTER WHAT SHE WEARS, IT'S always too much.

Every Saturday, the chaos on the street reaches extravagant heights. Regularly distracted by distant rumbling, Pauline comes to sit at the window, sidewalks exploding with color, people who walk slowly, stop, recognize each other, find themselves in a group of five or six at the corner of a building, shopping bags at their feet. And sometimes they come to blows, lose themselves in arguments, it can last a long time.

Just now, a particularly furious commotion, immediately she stations herself to see what's happening. A police car stops on rue des Poissonniers, two cops lead away a woman who was selling fabric on the hood of a car, people gather around, not happy, the woman doesn't want to be pushed around. The cops are nervous, even though there are already about ten of them, they feel like assholes anyway, hostile neighborhood, with too many people on the sidewalks. A glass is thrown from one of the windows. Pauline watches the street empty out, people distancing themselves slowly at first, then running, she knows from the stinging that they dropped tear gas, she closes the windows. It stinks all through the surrounding streets, that nasty odor of a fearful cop turned dangerous. In two minutes twenty of them show up, blue uniforms banding together, still not reassured but arrogant all the same. A guy with his kids comes to complain, all upset, they can't do that; they just hurl abuse at him. Pauline waits for the smell to fade before reopening her window and leaning outside again, like a lot of neighbors, and like a lot of them, she's watching the pigs below, wishing that someone would do something so that they'd be gone for good.

Lying on her stomach, she goes through her sister's mail.

Every morning, the super slips a few envelopes under the door. It's surprising, so many letters. Some are long, others simple notes, some of the handwriting is elegant, some gnarly or clumsy, some turns of phrase are touching, others are idiotic and make you want to laugh. But all the letters speak of love; they spoke to her sister of nothing else. And not only sex, as Pauline had imagined. Lovers or suitors, she'd amassed a nice collection.

The same woman who used to brag, "I know this guy, I earn this much, I go to this place," had omitted an entire facet of her life, never boasted, "If you knew how much they adore me," and yet that's really the only thing she could have boasted about however she liked. In a closet, Pauline found large cardboard boxes full of these letters, words of love or hostility, a lot of unopened, buried envelopes. Piled on top of each other, this blaze of lovers takes on strange accents, different handwritings. But certain passages, down to the last line, are the same, from one man to another, the same refrains appear, "And you won't be better off with anyone else," "You are afraid of love, you shouldn't be," phrases and then promises and tender threats, "I'll break down your door if you don't answer me," and stacks of harsh reproaches, "How can you do this to me," or else pitiful, "If you knew the state you've put me in," or menacing again, "You played me, now that I see you for what you are, I promise you, you'll pay."

And there's nothing chaste about these letters, even if they rarely admit it, her legs are magnificent, or else it's her eyes, then comes her chest or else her grace or her hair, then it's her hands that fascinate, bewitch, if not her strength or her fragility. Some of them evoke her warm pussy, treasure buried between her thighs. Nostalgia for that palace. She really knew how to hook them.

Each one takes her for himself, it's a given: she was made for the one writing to her. He wants her more than the others, he knows her, he can tell she needs him. And there are dozens like that, spread out over years, they are sure of that fact: she exists for them. And one by one, better than the others, each of them knows how to make her happy.

One phrase always reappears: "Why be afraid of happiness?" They are incapable of understanding why she would refuse such a blessing, to belong to them and to let them have their way with her. Incapable even of imagining that perhaps they disgust her, that they pile up like this, that perhaps she has good reason to be wary, that they always employ the same lines, from one man to the next, and always the same doggedness.

For some of them, perfectly candid, there is that drive to "have her," to be able to show off to all the other men in the city, so that they know who's boss, the one who's screwing the best broad, so that they get hard for him through her.

For others, just as candid, almost like she's their present, is that drive to transform her as they please, to turn her into their lifelong dream.

For all of them, in bursts, there's that stirring impatience, that obsessive imperative desire, to have her near them. There are lovely words, magnificent constructions concerning their love, sublime compliments. Each man sees his Claudine, describes her, magnified. Some of their projections are rather beautiful.

And others that are more sordid. And others that are too naive, they're exasperating.

But none of them, in the two days since she's gone through her mail, had the slightest suspicion that his missive might be filed away with so many others.

These cardboard boxes filled with letters imbue them with a particular tone.

Reading them all in one go, and seeing several arrive each day, slid under the door, and hearing certain voicemails left by certain men, Pauline imagines her sister as being assaulted from all directions. And these burning attentions that she aroused so frequently surrounded her in her solitude even more definitively than indifference.

That sadness, Pauline grasps for the first time, to be so desired, and to desire no one.

Someone rings the doorbell. Pauline approaches quietly, verifies through the peephole that it's Nicolas, and opens the door.

He asks, "What would you have done if it wasn't me?"

"I wouldn't have opened the door. It happened yesterday actually. A guy I had never seen."

"He didn't hear you come to look?"

"He did. I talked to him through the door, I said I wanted to be alone. He insisted, I told him I didn't have the keys, that I was locked inside, that he had to go. He kept insisting, so I insulted him, majorly, he took off."

Seeing the time, Nicolas proposes, "Let's go and buy groceries while it's not too crowded?"

"I don't feel like it. Let's order pizza."

"I'm sick of pizza, that American food is too greasy. You should get out a little, it'll do you good to get some fresh air. Then I have a lot of stuff to tell you."

He's already standing up, he's waiting for her to follow him.

Through the door of the supermarket, it's a little bit colder. A kid is crying, standing in a shopping cart, next to him his father is pretending not to hear him.

Nicolas tells Pauline what happened that morning at the office of the label they signed with.

A well-dressed gentleman is clumsily trying to fill a bag with apples; he must not be very good with his hands.

A woman fondles some apricots, grimacing.

Another woman sniffs the containers of meat, displaying a similar skeptical disgust.

A kid offers his Coke from KFC to everyone who passes.

Nicolas chooses the register that seems to have the shortest line.

Pauline asks for a simple confirmation, "So it's all good, they're going to transfer everything into the account? When do you think we'll get it?"

"No, in the end we decided to do it over multiple

transfers. Otherwise we risk blowing it all at once and then we'd regret it."

He delivered this bullshit in a tone of utter confidence.

"You didn't actually do that, did you?"

"I did. It'll be spread out over nine months, that way we can rest easy for a while. That amount seems enormous, but it goes so fast . . ."

A very old hunchbacked woman talks to herself behind them. Her cart is filled with cat food and chocolate puddings of all kinds. She is annoyed about something, she grumbles, her white hair looks like cotton candy.

A terrible scramble in Pauline's head. Spread out over nine months . . . She hadn't imagined for a second that he would have such a stupid fucking idea. He's smiling at everyone, there's champagne in his cart.

"What were you thinking doing that without asking me?"

"I discussed it with the boss this morning, he told me it was for the best. Since it was in our interest, I decided to—"

"It's amazing how subservient you can be . . . I swear, now that I know you, I have a much better understanding of why everything is going haywire—shit."

When she gets angry like this, she starts spinning around, fidgeting with her fingers. She looks around everywhere to avoid looking at him, like she's afraid that she wouldn't be able to stop herself from hitting him. She gets like this sometimes; he doesn't really understand where it comes from. She scares him a little when she gets so worked up, and it really pisses him off that he's forced to put up with it. So he waits for it to pass, for her to stop PMSing. She stammers another few insults, then decides,

"Anyway you can go fuck yourself with your stupid fucking ideas, I'm not going to do them any favors, I want my money up front and all at once. Tomorrow, you'll go and change the contract."

"Well, while we're at it, you can just shove it up your ass."

She sees that she's gone too far, gently changes tactic, "Shit, Nico, why did you do that without asking me?"

"Listen, sweetheart, all you had to do was come with me. It's been three months now that I've been dealing with these creeps on my own because madame doesn't deign to accompany me, three months that I've been in negotiations and on top of that I negotiate on my own, and today what I did you don't like. If I'm too much of a fucking idiot, you shouldn't have dragged me into this."

While speaking, Nicolas places his groceries on the belt. The cashier is always chipper, today he's singing a song by Lio. He brandishes a saucepan and asks his colleague if she knows how much it is.

Pauline murmurs, "I'll let you pay, I'll wait for you out front."

On the sidewalk, she wants to light a cigarette but can't find her lighter. A guy passes and says hello to her, she looks away. She wants to avoid crying because, after all, it might look suspicious.

She walked into this supermarket ten minutes ago. She was walking on air, everything was in place. Everything had unfolded as planned, like in a dream, a little more added to their payday. Nicolas had increased the offers, had handled it like a champ. Everything should have been transferred into an account opened specifically for that, supposedly it was more practical . . .

He arrives, hands full of bags. Timid smile, he hopes that she's calmed down. He's always conciliatory. As soon as she gets angry, for whatever reason, he takes it as a sort of hiccup, a thing that'll pass.

She holds out her hand to help him carry the bags. "Give me half."

He refuses. "It's fine, leave it."

She walks behind him, doesn't say another word. Nine monthly payments. It doesn't seem like anything anymore. Sébastien will get out in less than three months. It's funny how just one piece of news can make everything fall to pieces. Two, three words strung together incorrectly and everything is wiped out, destroyed.

Leaning against a wall, a man with gray hair is yelling into his cell phone, the whole street can hear him, he's bright red from anger, maybe he'll explode all over the sidewalk.

THE FAN OSCILLATES back and forth; Pauline always sits in front of it, enjoying its caresses.

Fifth beer she's taken from the fridge, she feels a little less out of sorts. She will find a way to change that ridiculous clause. It's like anything else, just a matter of patience.

Nicolas cuts onions into super-thin slices, like he saw the professional chefs do with garlic on *Goodfellas*. Every little thing takes him hours. She refrains from making any comment, since it's nice of him to prepare the food to begin with. But that doesn't stop it from annoying her, such ludicrous slowness to cut up three vegetables.

"We have to find a manager, for the concerts. Have you ever been on tour? I have the most intense nostalgia for being in a van. The kind of thing you don't appreciate until you have some distance. In the moment, mostly you think about how long a drive it is, how your seat is uncomfortable, and it's always the same asshole who speeds up just to cut you off. But years later, all that comes back to you are the hilarious memories, the stupid games you played."

He goes on and on about it, almost shaking with enthusiasm. She lets it happen and sits in front of the TV. She thinks, *I'm not going to see any of this, asshole, I'm going to squeeze all of that money out of you, one way or another, and I'm going to get myself far away from you, forget you immediately, and you, to console yourself for having been betrayed, you can just drive off in a van, since that seems to amuse you so much.*

Rumbling in the street, she leans out the window to see what's happening. It always takes a bit of time to understand, discern in the idle of the crowd who is mixed up with who, try to guess why . . . A canary has escaped, she can see it, frantic, flying around the whole street, it went crazy in its cage. Many hands reach out to try and catch him, the owner at her window yells something then signals that she's coming down.

Pauline returns to her seat, fingers the contract Nicolas brought back from the record label. She goes through it once more. There's no jargon or fine print that you might miss. Everything is black and white: I'm fucking you in every orifice. It's very, very clear. And the artist will do this and the artist will do that. And the label will become their owner and will do absolutely nothing except milk the cow and drink the milk.

Nicolas starts on a sauce, chucks in the tomatoes. Says everything he's doing out loud, "Don't put the gas on too high or else it'll burn." He does this every time he prepares a meal. Sometimes she feels really sorry for him, then dismisses it immediately: *It's not a good idea to act so blissfully ignorant, he's really asking for it.*

IT'S A PRETTY aggravating summer. The sky is white enough to strain your retinas and then all at once it changes, torrents of water crash against the windshield and around you everything becomes black as night waiting to fall.

Sébastien is glued to the car window, devouring the scenery, without really being able to tell if it's actually making him emotional or if he's faking it to match the idea he had of himself upon release. Forest to his left, trees stretched in one direction because of the wind, blowing strong.

There are other cars on the road which pass them regularly. A noise like mechanical waves. The car radio crackles, ruining all the bass lines, making a mess of the groove.

The man driving follows the other cars too closely. Idiot. A guy who used to come to the visiting room. That's his thing, he visits people. He's done time, too, a while ago though. He never wound up back there, but he didn't move on to another place in his life either. As soon as he got out, he understood that the link was broken between him and those who had never been there. He didn't have much respect for them anymore, he had the impression that they understood nothing, that they didn't know, and most importantly, that they had seen nothing. In fact he would talk only about that: the joint, the guards, the cell-mates, the schemes . . . He clings to it, his suffering, it's the crux of his soul.

He offered to bring Sébastien back in his car, it was really nice of him. That day, in the visiting room, Sébastien wasn't unhappy to see him, it was a special occasion.

Now out, it's almost annoying that he knows his driver. Marker on the side, Paris is ninety-three miles away. He has to be patient with his irritation.

How many times, way too many times, he's imagined this day. The world getting back into the swing of things, the world turning without him, rejoining it once again. Being outside. He must have set his expectations for free-dom too high.

Now it's just *this*: the lousy weather, the car that isn't moving and smells a little like feet.

It's perhaps this, precisely, that is so good. To be able to complain about the little, not-so-bad things that make up a part of life, be a little bothered without it turning into despair.

"So your girl's waiting for you in Paris?"

Bitterness at hearing this question. Sébastien apolo-gizes, "I don't really feel like talking. But I don't want you to take it the wrong way . . ."

"Of course, of course, I know what it's like, you know . . . I know."

But Pauline was not waiting for him there. He hadn't told her that he had gotten out, supposedly to surprise her. But if he was being honest with himself, it was to have two days. And he knows exactly what for, what he's had in mind all these weeks, exceedingly distinct images, mixed with memories, driving him insane. Each time it's the same thing, gradually growing worse.

Once he's done it, he'll feel even worse than he does now. He knows from experience. But even still, he can't help himself.

He pictures himself face down on the ground, his head being kicked in. He wishes someone would grab him and stick a rifle to his temple, shoot over and over. That would ease his conscience for being the way he is.

And he wishes he were there already.

"It's normal to be like that, you can't let it get to you," a guy from his cell had said, arms crossed behind his neck. He had talked with him for hours. He didn't need to explain in detail, he had understood in a matter of seconds. "The little girl in red we saw in the video the other day?" No attitude of salacious complicity, no dirty locker-room talk between men discussing the same hole. He had just shaken his head, resigned. "Everyone is like that, or else why would there be so many whores?" No one could argue with that.

PAULINE IS LEANING out her bedroom window.

A black sweater is lying there, a sleeve folded back, fallen on the sidewalk. A veiled woman crosses the street. A bike is attached to a pole that says WRONG WAY, it's been there for days, with no wheels. The grubby shutters opposite, the PMU LOTO MÉTRO signs at the tabac, fruits and vegetables at the grocery store, a guy sweeps out front, a baseball cap on his head. The passersby trace different lines, their trajectories never identical.

Nicolas left a minute ago. Much earlier than usual. Since she wouldn't speak another word, he ended up promising her, "I'll go see them as soon as possible to say we changed our minds and we want the money all at once." She had barely shaken her head, "Do what you want," as if that weren't the problem. Sudden attack of paranoia, she should never have taken a drag from the joint, it does this to her every time. Convinced he'll suspect something, even that he sees it coming. So she had carefully avoided the subject. She would talk to him about it again tomorrow, or after, stay prudent, don't rush anything. First, make sure he doesn't know anything. Then, only then, confirm that he'll really do what needs to be done. If she stays focused, everything will turn out the way she wants.

Telephone rings, three times, then the answering machine message, always the same, a beep and the voice starts, irritated, frantic.

She closes the curtains, goes back to her seat. The telephone starts ringing again. Bitter pang, pit of her stomach. She resolves to unplug the phone as soon as he's left his message, looks for the outlet along the baseboard. She barely listens to what's being said on the machine, but the name leaps into her eardrum.

"It's Sébastien, you there?"

"Yes, I'm here . . . But where are you?"

"I'm downstairs. Can I come up?"

"You're really downstairs?"

"Give me the code?"

She waits at the door, she doesn't understand how he could be outside, even less how he could have guessed that she was at her sister's. First she's scared. For him to see her in that outfit, and she doesn't have time to change. Is he going to think she's gone crazy? And what she's done, she thought she would never have to tell him about it. Will he be sad, disappointed? She's mad at herself for ruining this moment, this day when they're finally reunited, which should be light and cheerful.

She thinks of her made-up mouth. Bathroom, she wipes her lips with a towel, looks in the mirror, too much makeup for him, way too much. But already he's ringing the doorbell. She hurries to the door.

In his arms. This body that she knows entirely, nothing forgotten, they are buried in each other, it's like breathing again.

Grateful that he takes her in his arms first, and stays pressed against her for a long time, before asking questions. That he doesn't judge anything before hearing from her own mouth what's going on. All she can say is, "It's so good to see you again."

Then come brusque gestures, desire fed by so much waiting, it's an explosion. He takes her in his arms like he's never done before, similarly driven mad by all this time without her.

"Come on, Claudine, let's go to your room."

He takes her by the hand, leads her without hesitation toward the bedroom.

She follows him. It starts from her nose then mouth throat middle of her chest and down to the bottom of her stomach, scraping through her from end to end. The heart of a machine pounds in the middle of her, a collapse that carries away everything, nothing left standing, she is shattered against the ground, each limb smashed and bones nearly crumbling.

She says nothing. In the bedroom he sits on the bed, looks at her, wild animal gleam in his eyes, and he half smiles at her, a brutal joy, gently coaxes her toward him.

"I've been waiting for this moment for so long, Claudine."

She lets it happen. Convinced he'll realize his mistake on his own. She waits. Too embarrassed to intervene.

She lets herself be manipulated. He undresses her with care, very slowly. Each part of her body that he discovers he devours attentively with his eyes, his fingers, then his mouth and tongue. This face, she's never seen it before. Run through with a frenetic energy, joy bursts in his pupils, consumed with rage.

She should have said something earlier. Now the moment has passed. She doesn't want for everything that will happen to happen. She doesn't want to know more. But she still lets herself be worshipped, like she's being dissected.

What we don't know about the other. All that he hid.

She is lying on her back. He's on his knees next to her. With one hand, he holds out the head of his cock for her to suck. The other hand is plastered against her breasts, he kneads them so feverishly that he hurts her a little and when she tries to free herself she feels his cock shove into her mouth even more violently, his arousal upped a notch.

He makes her change position, regularly, wordlessly. He grabs her to show her how he wants it now. She feels like an amusement park unto herself. She's on all fours, he corrects her arch, bangs against her guts until he's striking at her core. He spreads her ass wide, she glances over her shoulder, he is fascinated by the haunch he's massaging, at his disposal. His gaze turns serious, as if he were about to descend into a pit of snakes.

She feels like a fly on the wall. She feels the in and the out, the hand spanking her ass. But it's like she's not there, witnessing it from afar. She thinks of other things, of what she'll say after, of how comfortable he is having sex with her. She thinks, *He fucks my sister, he's used to it. And she makes him like this, completely nuts, unrecognizable.* Never has she had this effect on him. He didn't like for her to take him in her mouth, he would slide his hand under her chin and bring her back up right away, with a little embarrassed smile. "I don't really want you to do that to me."

He puts her on her back again. Brings her thighs around both sides of his neck, he starts very gently, going in and out of her, his eyes riveted to her breasts. It's impossible, to look at her the way he looks at her, and not realize right away. Then he speeds up, smashes into her methodically, now he's looking only at her breasts swinging in every direction and the more they shake the harder he rams into her. It burns, it's almost painful, he's thrusting so fast.

Her mind is still elsewhere—*Did he come to see her often?*—while she feels her body (it wouldn't be right to say despite herself, since she didn't even think to resist, it was all so inconceivable) respond to his advances. He slows down the tempo, her pelvis raised up and his two hands knotted into her back, bringing him deep inside her. He raises his head, like a sprinter near the finish line, she hears him say, "So, slut, no matter how long it takes, I can always make you come." And she moans. For a period of time that she'll later be unable to quantify, she is given over completely to her sex, something inside her that she didn't know existed before opens up, an entire space, vast, sensitive, absorbing, made up of a thousand fractures.

He stops breathing, apnea, he's soaked with sweat, then he humps her like a madman.

She comes back to herself, breaks away again, mentally, from the woman performing. He lets out a sort of growl. The one that she knows, the one he always makes. But with her it's a little wheeze and today it's a loud roar. Finally collapses onto her. Falls over. His body is damp, a bit too heavy. She gently extricates herself, he asks, "You want me to pull out already?" She nods yes, she slides to the side.

He likes to stay inside for a while after the act with Pauline, too.

He grabs one of her breasts, kisses it, and murmurs, "I'm crazy about your tits." He smiles, then gets up to go rinse off.

He's also used to doing that, cleaning off his cock at the sink and even checking himself out a little.

She hears him singing at the top of his lungs, from the other side of the wall, "I'm completely crazy about you," clowning around.

He knew exactly where the bathroom was. He's at home here.

He pokes his head through the door.

"I'm a little hungry, can I take a look around?"

"Help yourself."

"Don't move, I'll be right back."

She is stretched out, her arms spread-eagled. She'll have to talk eventually. She knows this sensation well, when her sister takes what matters most to her. It's an old routine that doesn't happen so often anymore; she thought she had escaped it. Now that it's returned, it's familiar, there's nothing pleasant about it but it's certainly hers.

She gets up without him seeing, she watches him in the kitchen. He makes coffee, he knows where the filters are and what metal tin to open, the one with the sugar.

She lies down again. He comes back with a tray full of food. He's beaming. He sits next to her, kisses her neck. "So that's it, I'm really out. Until I got to your place it hadn't really sunk in . . . But now I'm outside."

And he extends his arms as if to take full advantage of the space and all that breathable air. Then he leans toward her. "How many times did I make you come?"

As though it were a question he asked often. Pauline coaxes him against her, tears filling her eyes now, and she kisses him as she would if it were just the two of them. He pushes her away, a bit surprised, but without losing any of his good humor. "Hang on, I'm super hungry. We'll go back to that after."

And he laughs. "Let me regain some of my strength first at least . . ."

He eats, talks, without realizing that she hasn't even moved. Her throat is too tight for her to get out a single word.

He talks about her. "I've got to call Pauline tomorrow, before I leave. Have you had any news from her?"

She shakes her head no. He swallows the last bite of his sandwich. "Are you guys fighting?"

She's intrigued by the question. She still can't manage to say what she needs to say.

He gets back in bed, lies against her. Immediately she remembers how she missed his body and presence while she slept. That he is everything for her, her only comfort in the world. She feels his hand sliding right between her legs. She moves away, he pulls her back, he laughs. "Are you trying to turn me on even more or what? Quit your games, I bet you're all wet."

"Stop it."

She straightens up and lights a cigarette, clears her throat as if trying to strengthen her voice. She says, without even planning to, "Madame Lentine, you know, the cool neighbor, she died all of a sudden."

He waves his hand to signal that he doesn't really care. "She was an old woman after all. Pauline told you that?"

She smiles, as if it were a stupid question.

"I don't share stories about our neighbor with Claudine. You know I don't talk much. She fell in the street. Dead."

He grimaces the way he does when he doesn't really like a joke.

"You've never pulled this trick on me before. And I suggest you don't do it again."

She rubs her eye, acts as if she didn't hear him. She continues.

"Also, those assholes from the building management company never sent anyone to replace the water heater. I lost my mind every day turning the hot water tap. They're idiots, seriously, idiots—"

He grabs her by the arm. She doesn't know this face either, like he could slap her.

"Knock it off, Claudine. If there's something you want us to talk about, you spit it out, whatever you have to say to me . . . But you don't joke about that."

He nearly breaks her wrist, she lowers her eyes.

"I didn't really know how to tell you. I took her place two months ago."

JULY 14. KIDS going ballistic with firecrackers. Three days of this. Nonstop explosions, more or less jarring. At the beginning, it's startling—"Was that a gunshot?"—and then you get used to it, like with anything, pretty quickly too.

Lying on her bed, at the end of the afternoon, the curtains in the bedroom still drawn. The mattress springs cut into her back in big, hard circles. She stays for entire days like that, doing nothing but listening to the answering machine going off, the people arguing in the street, the kids playing in the stairwell. Their mother calls, they don't listen, she has to go over and smack them. Pauline stays there, drinks tea drowned in milk, lights cigarettes, turns onto her stomach to smoke them.

One image stands out from the rest, deploys itself very distinctly, makes itself more urgent than the present. She's on all fours on the bed, he still has his white T-shirt on, he had her lie down on her back to suck him off with her head bent back. She blinks her eyes to make it pass, to not think of anything, to block it out, clear away that distinct sensation. Each time, she feels herself tense, as though she had bit into a lemon. That terrific shame, reddish black, towering over her.

Her brain is malfunctioning again, it transmits the image to her one more time, same as before, he spreads her thighs wide and guides her hand so that she touches herself, his eyes riveted to her. Fascinated by her crotch.

She turns her head toward the wall, as if to physically make the image fuck off and haunt someone else.

Layers of emotions cohabiting the same body, but at

war with each other. Anger and feeling destroyed, a lack of him and of shame, relief, a heavy sadness.

Her nails are unclean, uneven lengths, a bit of black underneath. She gets up to wash her hands, the white soap lathers, smells good, she lets the warm water run over her hands.

The telephone, again, a nauseating pang. Sébastien calls nonstop, doesn't leave messages but doesn't hang up.

He comes and rings her doorbell, she freezes when she hears it, her heart pounds at full throttle, she doesn't want to open the door. She waits for him to leave.

Now everything is stupid, everything meaningless, a world full of ants.

When she told him, he had hesitated for a moment. Before speaking, he put on his Bénard pants, his T-shirt. A strange precaution.

She took advantage of his silence.

"The best thing would be for you to leave. The keys to our place are at Armand's. I'll write to you once you're there."

"Wait, wait . . . I'd like to understand what's going on, at least."

"I've already understood too much. We'll finish this another time, okay?"

Shoving his bag into his hands, she pushed him toward the entryway. He let himself be pushed. She could feel his distress, and she wanted a lot of things in this world but what she wanted most was for him not to go. Still, she opened the door, avoided his eyes, and waited for him to leave. She was dying to hold him back and act as if nothing out of the ordinary had happened. When he was in the stairwell, she leaned over the banister to yell, "And bravo on the pelvic thrusting, asshole, I had no idea you were so talented."

Door slam.

She is seated on the couch. In fact, she wasn't surprised. The most incredible things tend to veil themselves in absurdity. Never had she actually suspected, *Did he go see my sister?*

But now that she knows, she can remember when it began and even list the dates of his visits. And her mind had always made sure, unbeknownst to her, not to make the connections, not to realize. Above all, not to know.

And so that's how it was.

It didn't happen right away. Of course, the first few weeks that Sébastien and Pauline were together, her sister did what she always did: hovered around him. When she had to lean over to get something next to him, she happened to be wearing a low-cut shirt. When he would talk about a band that he really liked, would you believe it—"How funny!"—and her eyes would sparkle as she said it—that was her "fave" group. If he was talking about a country that he wanted to visit—"That's crazy, Pauline told you!"— that's where she wanted to go too, and for a while now. And she had small gifts for him, books to give him, a tape to lend him, a film he had to see.

That was her little game. Not entirely devised to piss off Pauline, to steal her boyfriend. She did it as soon as any man was in her vicinity. An anxiety took hold of her that she absolutely needed to subdue. She needed to exist, at least in his eyes, the curve of an erection, to verify that she was really there.

And until Sébastien, her strategy had always worked.

One day, they weren't yet fifteen years old, Pauline remembers well, it was her first real relationship. With a sweet and sad boy who seemed entirely made for her. They had already been together a few weeks. In her parents' garden, a white plastic table with rickety chairs. The boy didn't seem to be falling for her trap, he seemed not even to realize, or to care. Claudine lost her head, exasperated, she ended up sighing, "Fuck it's hot out," and took off her T-shirt, looking him right in the eye, a whore's smile. He turned red, looked away. She lay down on the grass, she touched her breasts as if it were natural, she stroked herself in front of him, flaunted herself.

A little while later, almost night, they were talking, Pauline heard her say, "I like to have sex with much older men, because they know all about women . . ."

When she hadn't yet slept with anyone. The boy didn't know what to say, he ended up suggesting to Pauline, "Let's take a walk into town?"

She left them alone for about five minutes, the time it took to go upstairs and throw on a sweater and brush her hair. Through her bedroom window, without meaning to, she saw them. Claudine was lying on the table and he was between her legs, pants around his ankles.

Pauline lingered for a few minutes. When she went back downstairs the boy had left and her sister had shrugged her shoulders. "He got tired of waiting for you. And anyway he's kind of lame, isn't he?"

He was the very first guy she had sex with.

And from that day on, Pauline found it normal for her

sister to devour all her guys. She had what Pauline didn't, she had what men needed.

So Pauline willingly brought each new boyfriend home, for him to meet her sister, and for him to leave with her—until Sébastien, the first guy to not want the other twin.

With him, Claudine had quickly abandoned her efforts. They got along terribly. It was rare to leave them seated in the same room without returning to them fighting.

Claudine exasperated him. "Can't she ever shut her mouth? That stupid bitch just likes to provoke people. And on top of it she's ugly, she's a two-dollar whore."

The first two years, Claudine and Sébastien rarely crossed paths, and nothing happened.

And then Pauline left for an internship. The first night she called the house everything was fine except the car. It didn't want to start anymore, nothing he could do about it, and Sébastien was temping far out in the suburbs at the time. He was pretty upset; for once he had found work and he couldn't go, and he had already tried all his friends, no one could lend him their car.

"Call Claudine."

"No."

"Stop being so against her. You're just borrowing her ride, not going on vacation with her."

"I'll see . . . I'll figure it out in any case. Shit, the one time I have a job."

After that, when she called, he was never there.

When she came back, she asked, "Where were you every night? You never picked up." Just asking, just curious. And that pissed him off. "I was here, there, can't I go have a drink without filling out a form for you?"

He also said, "In the end, Claudine helped me out with the car."

"Did you guys argue?"

"No, no . . . your sister's changed, she's not such a cunt anymore. I have to go back to her place, by the way. Since she did me a favor, I told her I would change her headlight. I'll probably go Monday."

"That's too bad, I have work Monday, I won't be able to go."

"Yeah, but if I don't go then I'll never have the time."

And everything was the same as before, except for several weeks when he didn't let her kiss him when she passed him at home. It bothered him. "Don't you ever get sick of being glued to my side?" He said it like he'd been sick of it for months, whereas he had always been affectionate before. She got on his nerves for no reason.

At the time, she told herself that he was irritable because he couldn't find work. He had little unpleasant outbursts.

Now she understands, these scenes would happen, inevitably, just after he had spent the night out with his friends: "You think we have two drinks and then go home to sleep? No, we drink all night and talk about the entire world and how it should be put back together."

And then it was done. The two lovers had stopped seeing each other.

She also remembers when Claudine left for Paris, her going-away party, to celebrate. Sébastien refused to go, it was Pauline who had insisted, "We never go out anywhere together. Come on, we'll stop by, just long enough to have a drink, see some people, and say goodbye to her."

"I don't want to."

"Please."

But she didn't feel well when they got there, a sudden headache. She had taken Sébastien aside. "I'm going home, you should stay."

"I'm coming with you."

"Stay, I'm just going to go to sleep right away, stay here and have fun."

He came home the next morning, without a word. From then on, very precisely, a terrible despair began working its way into their relationship.

Then the trips there. He would go to Paris for "business." He never said that he had seen Claudine.

But now she knows, every time he came back it made him sick, physically sick, sore throats or toothaches or other delightful things, every time he came back.

Except everything was going well between them. So she didn't want to know anything. To have to change anything.

THE TELEPHONE AGAIN. Nicolas, in a tiny quiet voice, "I don't want to overload your answering machine, but I'm on the verge of panic, wondering what's going on with you . . ."

Pauline picks up, for the first time in three days. "I needed some rest. How are you?"

"A lot better now that I hear your voice."

"Can't I have a few quiet days without having to justify myself? What horrible thing did you imagine happened to me?"

"That you had become friendly, all of a sudden. I missed you yelling at me, I got too used to it."

Pauline pretends to laugh at his dumb sense of humor. Maintains the illusion that everything's going pretty well between them, even though she's still resentful.

But through pretending, it's become a reflex. She forgets to remember that she doesn't find him funny, that she isn't happy to hear from him, that she has no desire to see him. The responses come out on their own, sometimes she even forgets that she's doing it on purpose.

Nicolas clears his throat, adopts an annoyed tone, "There are some things we need to talk about . . ."

Burst of mounting adrenaline: of course he suspects something, enormous exploding panic, her chest shatters. Block it all, sealed mask. Keep acting like someone who has nothing to be ashamed of. She proposes, "Want to hang out tonight?"

He accepts. Unassuming, ask questions to find out more, discern the reasons to be worried. She inquires, "It seems like something's wrong, is it something bad or what?"

"Not pleasant. But nothing to worry about either. I'll come over around eight? I won't stay long, I have a party to go to after."

"Oh yeah? I'll go with you."

Brief silence at the other end, then Nicolas sighs. "For three months I've been pestering you to come out with me, and it's today you decide to!"

"That's the point, it's getting old not seeing anyone. Why is today worse timing than yesterday? Just to piss me off?"

"We'll see each other soon, we'll talk. I bet you won't want to come with me anymore."

"You never know . . ."

He laughs a little, obviously fake, disgusted, hangs up.

She doesn't know what to think. Leans toward the option: *False alarm, he wants to talk to me about something else.* But without losing sight of another possibility: *He's being deceitful in reassuring me, really trying to corner me tonight.* Overestimate the enemy, always think he's capable of being as clever as you are. Sometimes they only pretend to be stupid . . .

She needs to find the willpower to go to this party with him tonight. She has absolutely no desire. Except that she has to get out of here. Break the cycle with Sébastien at its core, force herself to be distracted, cut herself off from her delirium.

She wants Sébastien to be there, to hurl insults at him.

She repeats them on loop, all the reproaches she has for him. She yells them out loud, as if he were there. Relief, immediately followed by a renewed frustration that exacerbates the wound. Vaguely aware of the pain, Pauline knows that she has to go about things differently. Incapable of doing the right thing, she is tortured, distorted by the sullied desire to go back to him, to revel in what hurts. Like an alcoholic who knows that it makes them violent, that they shouldn't drink, even they, frankly, would prefer not to do it. But if you leave a bottle next to their bed, they'll drink it. Inevitably.

Her own bottle is full of regrets, remorse, sorrow at being abandoned. She can't stop herself, it's so full, she'll drink from it. Inevitably.

She shouldn't have been there. This pain, like the whole world is cruelly collapsing around her. These things, so tangible, that should never have disappeared, become elusive all at once, turn against us.

Why did she have to be there? She's the one who asked for it, she's the one who didn't warn Sébastien. It is, in the end, her fault that everything has gone to hell.

And when he fucked her like a whore, she, also, started moaning. And he heard her.

Both of them, face to face, expressing things that should have remained secret.

She puts on her makeup in front of the mirror. She thinks of Nicolas, when she first arrived, giving her advice and showing her the girls in magazines. She's looking forward to seeing him, it surprises her. She's impatient for him to arrive, for him to recount his silly stories.

Thinking about the notorious advance, she suddenly has an idea, the only idea that makes sense now: she will actually make the album.

Rather than barricading herself in with the money all alone with no desire to go anywhere, she will stay in this apartment, they'll work in the studio over the summer. They'll record something good, together.

The advantage of innocence is that it allows others to make mistakes without causing suffering, and it leaves them the time to recuperate.

She concentrates and applies her lipstick, outlining the

upper lip without going over the edge. Then she finds the color disgusting, takes it off right away. She opens all the tubes, one by one, trying to find the right one.

Out loud, to herself, she comments, "But if we do it for real, one or two things will have to change . . ."

She had let him make all the decisions, thinking it was all a joke. He has pretty shitty taste, eccentric ideas, except everyone else has the same ones. For the title and the sleeve, for certain parts of the tracks.

She takes stock, mentally, of all the things she had let slide when she still thought . . .

She looks at herself in the mirror; she's ready. She did everything as required, it took her all afternoon.

The nails to paint, the legs to shave, the calluses on her heels to smooth, the hair to wash and dry while fighting to make it straight, the armpits to shave, the foundation to apply, the eyes to line, the body to perfume. Everything needs tampering, you have to be careful.

Then choose what goes best with her body, with the weather, with the fashion, with the occasion.

Now she looks at herself, and she thinks she looks okay.

Spinning around in every direction, to see herself from behind, in profile, verify that everything looks good, she observes, "It could be great, to record an album."

She even feels stupid not to have thought of that before.

HE RINGS THE doorbell at eight on the dot. Six-pack of beer in hand, he puts them directly in the fridge to keep them cold.

"You're not very talkative today."

He's still trying to be a smartass, but it's clear he's nervous. Very visibly, he would have preferred to find someone else to bring her up to speed. Pauline lets him sort himself out, gather momentum, and get out what he has to tell her that's so unpleasant. She already knows that it won't be: "So, you little whore, your plan was to ditch me and take off with the advance?" because his embarrassment is real.

He sits down and opens a can. She turns on the TV and starts to flip through the channels. She lands on a black-and-white film, a baker who's lost his wife. It's the end of the story, she comes back. A priest lectures her. Then he sends her back to her husband, who is very nice to her. Pauline is fascinated. Not even sad. It comes back to her, all the times she's seen people cry in those circumstances, or else make themselves sick: "I can't stop picturing them together . . ." Why is it so painful when everyone goes through it?

The baker takes it out on the cat, and his wife is in tears. She seems to regret it. Pauline comments, "She's lucky, to have a husband like that. He's incredibly nice."

Nicolas isn't convinced.

"Maybe she would have been better off if she'd stayed in the cave with her stud. In any case, girls never like that, guys who are nice to them. Unless you tear them down first. Then it pays off to be the nice guy."

"Stop talking nonsense and let me watch the end of the movie."

"You've never seen it?"

It's the fear of infidelity, in the modern sense of the term. What's broken, between her and Sébastien, is all the trust she had in those things she knew about him, things that never changed, that she really liked. All the respect for the man she thought he was. Her trust must have weighed heavily on him. Those ideas she had, that she stuck to him, and don't you dare change, or else you'll have nothing. And that's the reason she put up with it, let it happen, as long as he lied. As long as he kept up with the fantasy she imposed on him.

Credits, she flips through the channels again. Nicolas brings over two beers. Movie trailer, a guy breaks everything in an office. He screams, "I waited for her all night!" A friend tries to calm him. The furious guy explains, "I asked her, 'Are you cheating on me?' She responded, 'Took you long enough to realize.'" Pauline declares, "It's a conspiracy! Did you set this up?"

"Why, what's going on, are you being cheated on?"

She keeps flipping, without responding. Making more and more stupid mistakes, what came over her to make her say that? No matter what, never talk to him about Sébastien. Fortunately, Nicolas is absorbed enough in whatever he has to say that he doesn't ask any more questions.

On the TV, a black guy wearing star-shaped glasses and platform boots sings and writhes in every direction. Cameras film girls dancing from behind, direct close-ups under their butts. Pauline asks, "So what's going on with you? Usually, when we see each other, I can barely breathe you talk so much."

"I'm not in the same mood as I usually am."

"I'm not complaining. I prefer it when you're quiet, actually . . ."

She thought that would get him started. He likes silly conversations, he's good at the back-and-forth. But tonight he pauses. Ends up remarking, "You've improved your sense of humor since last time . . . At least I was use-ful for something."

He says it jokingly, trying to keep his dignity, but he's visibly depressed. So Pauline decides to facilitate things for him.

"'At least I was useful for *something*?' What's that sup-posed to mean?"

"I screwed things up a little."

Another few seconds of not daring to say it, a sheepish look comes over him, he probably knows it suits him, has used it often. He hits her with it all at once.

"It's all bullshit, we don't have a record label or a pub-lisher, no one wanted to sign us, so we don't have an advance, actually we don't have anything more than the day we first met. I lied to you, I don't really know why, since it was obvious that you would find out eventually . . ."

Then he stops talking, looks all around the apartment attentively as if he were there to fix things, the windows, the ceiling, the sink. Leaves Pauline the time to take in what he's just told her.

She asks for clarification, "How long have you been lying to me?"

Trying to assess the damage, rapid inventory, in case there might be anything at all to salvage . . . He's in a truly pitiful state, but not crushed with remorse: now that he's spit it out, he could laugh.

He recaps, "Right after the concert, everyone was down, we were in business. But then, rapidly, we started to bomb. Monday there were five people who wanted to sign us. Next Monday they had no time for me. You should have come with me. I'm not saying that to exonerate myself, I'm saying it because it's obvious: if you had come with me, they wouldn't have switched off like that. That's when I started to lie about things when I came to see you. At first only a little bit: when a guy told me, 'I would need to see her perform,' I said to you, 'He needs to discuss the budget with the guy in charge.'"

"Your 'a little bit' is making me scared for the 'a lot' to come."

"It's been nearly a month since anyone took my calls."

"Why did you tell me a week ago that we had signed a contract?"

"I think it's my megalomaniac side. Honestly it's so nice to tell you, even if now you know I lied, it feels so good . . . I had good intentions, I was completely convinced that one day or another everything would work out."

"Where did you get the money that you gave me, then?"

"I took it from my mom. Don't worry about her, she won't miss it at the end of the month."

"Why are you telling me the truth now?"

"I decided to tell you the other night, when you took the news of the monthly installments so badly. That brought me back down to earth. I couldn't string you along like that for years."

"I've had enough of people telling me the truth, to be blunt, I'd rather people lie."

"Well, you should know it's the same for me. If I hadn't been sure it was going to end badly, I could have kept this up for another ten years before getting sick of it."

He goes looking for two more beers, rediscovers his cheeriness, continues, "Seriously, this situation was perfect for me. You, shut in here, always there when I stopped by. I come over, I tell you whatever I want, I show off for two or three hours. After, I give you two or three pieces of advice on how to dress, behave, do your makeup."

He asks her, in the voice of someone who knows that he'll be forgiven for everything, "Are you mad at me?"

"No. I think you're ridiculous, dishonest, and pathetic. But I can't pretend that I'm surprised. And this party tonight, are we actually invited or is that also part of your grand scheme?"

"No, I have invites. We're not blacklisted yet."

"We're just lightly disgraced, is that it?"

"We went out of style pretty fast."

The truth was that, more than anything, he quickly got tired of taking care of all the contract bullshit. He took it seriously for two or three days, convinced that he could make the effort. But a leopard can't change its spots. His natural state of being is not caring about anything. In rapid succession, he forgot about an appointment with one guy, showed up high to a meeting with a second, responded badly to a third. He screwed it all up in no time at all. And it didn't surprise him, or eat away at him.

She goes to the fridge, crouches down. "Did we already finish all the beer?"

"I'll go buy some if you want."

"Okay. While you're out I'll change my dress."

"That one's nice, it looks good on you."

"It's not flashy enough. This is a dress you wear when you've already signed a contract."

He follows her into her room, uneasy.

"What kind of thing are you thinking of wearing?"

"An astronaut suit, everyone will think it's glamorous."

She rifles through the heap of dresses. Raises her head, surprised that he's still on the doorstep.

"Can I get naked without you being here?"

"Okay. I'll go out. From day one I've found you unpredictable. But I mean that as a compliment."

It's hard to believe how well she's taking the news. Closing the door behind him, he thinks to himself that it's stupid—we have these lies we maintain that we think are so terrible, and once we reveal them it doesn't come as a surprise to anyone. While other things that we thought were insignificant trigger huge catastrophes.

She puts on a series of dresses and looks at herself. Puts aside the ones that she likes. She's picked up a few tricks about what makes an impression and what dazzles.

"Well this is just fantastic, this little piece of news."

She thought she was making a joke but it was the truth: she had lost everything that she had, everything that she was. Now it's all behind her. She has a hunger for everything that's still to come. Now that she's a new her.

Phone rings. The call doesn't end but no one says anything on the answering machine. It cuts off when the machine deems that it's been long enough. The phone rings again immediately after. She unplugs it.

Her good mood and big dreams deflate all at once.

TAXI, BARELY OUT of Paris, they drive through the middle of trees and grass, the smell of vegetation. For the first time, Pauline feels homesick. For places without twelve thousand cars, where you can see large stretches of clear sky. Her city, where people have an aperitif in the local bar, meet up frequently, without even calling, giving any heads-up, confirming. And on top of that, without getting angry at each other, doubting each other, judging each other.

Barely arrived at the party, she regrets wearing such a dress. Eyes on her, on the sly or blatantly, don't mean her any good.

It hits her in a few seconds: it must be a big joke. Cameras hidden in the bushes. Gathering of caricatures, losers, and swindlers of all ages.

Around her: "Oh my dear, how beautiful you look!" and then grimacing and bursts of laughter at nearly every step, people thrilled to see her, boisterous. A lot of old men, rather overexcited on the whole. "Nooo? You don't know so-and-so? Come quickly, I'll introduce you." They don't like each other. They all want pieces of the same pie, so they have to rub shoulders, but they have nothing in common besides the desire for profit, not their senses of humor, religions, convictions, or origins. Nothing brings them together and nothing makes them enjoy being together. They find themselves there out of obligation, hostile and uneasy. But they keep their eyes on the prize: the first person to touch my piece, I'll kill them.

It's a classy fucking reception, with a lake right in the middle and pretty barges floating on it, buffets of assorted colors, open bar, a lot of young and well-dressed girls to garnish the whole thing with a bit of vice.

Pauline and Nicolas hadn't yet managed to get a drink at the bar it was so crowded, and it's too funny to see how all these well-dressed people act like animals as soon as there's a buffet involved. She warns him, "You're going to find me painfully unpredictable, but I'm not staying longer than ten minutes."

"As you like. I'll go back with you, if you want."

It's always the same story: by her fifth drink she feels better. She's less determined to leave, she says things to the people who pass, who turn out to be pretty cool. Though a bit stymied. Something is blocking their throats, nothing comes out directly.

The cream of the business elite who have work, money, lives that people think are so sophisticated. They only sparkle when seen from a distance.

A guy has just arrived who stops Nicolas. "So, that demo?"

"No news."

But the guy isn't listening to his response, he intrudes, "And the young lady here with you, don't you want to introduce us?"

He looks at Pauline, undresses her with his eyes. Nicolas, anticipating her rejection of this man, gears up for a laugh.

But another Pauline emerges. Completely affable. Knowing her well, Nicolas can grasp, between two smiles, a small mean glimmer in her eye; she'll rip him to shreds on the spot.

Even when the guy deploys his CV, as if to say, "I have ways of having you, you know," she remains civil and charming. Though not wielding the weapon of discreet flattery, which Claudine swore was essential to any seduction, Pauline shows herself to be just as capable of hooking the gentlemen. Using a slightly cold distance, a paradox given her outfit. It suits her well.

Now that they've been introduced, the guy positions himself gradually and consciously with his back to Nicolas, quickly excluding him and busying himself with the lovely lady. He chats her up shamelessly, "We've never seen you in the office. Nicolas always came alone . . ."

"I thought that you were going to have us make an album, and that we'd have plenty of time to see each other . . ."

"That hasn't been ruled out, by the way! I'm very, very interested in what you do. You have a very rare gift."

Nicolas walks away from them, crossing his fingers that this asshole neglects to recount in detail his most recent visit to the record label. He'd smoked some excellent skunk beforehand, and found himself sniggering like an idiot right as they introduced him to the big boss. The boss had extended a virile hand, all business, booming, "I hope that you two will soon join our family," which set off a little laugh that nothing could restrain. Nicolas left the premises doubled over, running away without even saying goodbye.

Before he's out of earshot, he hears the fat oaf say very subtly and very originally, "With eyes like yours, you should really come out to talk business . . ."

And catches the smile Pauline blessed him with in response.

Nicolas remarks to himself, "When she starts acting, you're in big trouble, boys."

Fireworks. It's late now. Nicolas doesn't know the time, but given how wasted he is, he's probably been wandering around for a while.

A brunette playing the predictable femme fatale has taken up residence at his side. At first he racked his brain trying to remember where he knows her from. Without any luck. She wriggles next to him, as women like to do, her shoulder grazing his and even her hips seeking him out. Yet he feels that if he were to make a move on her, she would recoil, alarmed: "That's not at all what I had in mind." It discourages him every time, even ends up putting him in a bad mood. She wants him to screw her, it's obvious right off the bat. But you don't know what else she wants, which makes things so complicated.

So he lets her twist and turn. Remains available, a bit curt, tender at other moments. He knows girls like this from experience. They always end up cracking. When they're tired of moving closer for little touches—just so they can say, "What the hell is your problem?"—they jump right on him.

That's when he pulls a David Lynch on them. Once he can slip his hand between their thighs without a struggle, make them stammer, "I want you to fuck me," he steps aside for kicks, apologizing, "Some other time, I can't right now."

He only goes all the way with easy girls. They're the only ones who get him hard. Because they're ready to have sex in ten seconds, simply because they want to, without looking to profit from it.

He's had this compulsion since he was little, from having grown up with his very beautiful mother and two sisters. Their conversations as stupid and vicious as they can be when someone mistakes their ass for a tool of twisted power.

The brunette is telling him about her breasts, which her ex paid for. She wants him to look at them, she's even prepared to let him touch them.

It pushes girls pretty far in no time, a guy who remains unmoved in the face of their charms. There are some who would tear their hair out in frustration.

In the background, Pauline enters his field of vision. People are lined up to watch things explode in the sky. She's next to the big boss. They've been talking for quite a while now.

Well played, Nicolas thinks, because the gentleman is not easy to deal with. He watches her from a distance.

She has Claudine's body. An amusement park for men, her pussy full of magic and wonder. But, not very used to male company, she forgets to simper and show off the goods. It's an irresistible flaw, a black hole.

Someone comes looking for the boss, pulls him discreetly by the sleeve, wants him to accompany them somewhere, slips a couple of words into his ear. The boss signals yes, okay, then turns back toward Pauline, and, before taking his leave, writes something down for her. Probably his direct line. Then hands her the piece of paper and she writes something too, probably her phone number.

Right away, another guy monopolizes her.

Seeing this, the little bit of guilt he was able to conjure up vanishes. Nicolas feels relieved. It's not so bad that he screwed everything up with the labels. Not so bad, either, that he has absolutely no desire to spend hours glued to a computer mixing more beats. That girl there will take care of everything without him. She has a talent for making an impression.

More capable than Claudine was of clearing a path for herself to "the inside." Partly because of the anger she's not afraid to whip out, while her sister bottled it, let it fester, preferred to keep it banging around her guts rather than bare her teeth.

Also partly because Pauline keeps a cool head. She takes compliments like something owed, a slightly nauseating token. She shows no sign of knowing that men find her attractive, she doesn't lose sight of what she wants. She doesn't expect anything from the attention of others; she despises them too much.

He watches her off to the side, listening to what they say to her and responding vehemently, she must not agree. People around her raise their heads, surprised, now she's really getting angry. Then they start to laugh, complicit. They embrace her.

The asshole who whisked her away earlier comes back to join Nicolas. He catches him watching her.

"Fuck she's hot . . ."

Nicolas doesn't say anything.

The other guy continues pensively, "Too bad she's such a cunt, huh?"

Then he turns toward the brunette, and Nicolas takes the opportunity to go for a walk.

Later on in the party, he recognizes the small group she's with, she seems perfectly at ease with them. She's managed to pull the wool over the eyes of Claudine's friends the entire time. They passed each other at the buffet, Nicolas asks her, "Everything going okay?" She responds, "The worse the lie, the better it goes over." Contempt protects her from everything.

She leaves the party with them. Nicolas watches her walk away. She doesn't even look for him, doesn't even think of him. That hurts a little, but he knows he's already had his revenge: *If you'd come to see me, I could have told you where you were going.*

NIGHT, CAR, SHE'S completely wasted. She finds Paris really beautiful. She's even a little emotional.

They were supposed to drop her off at her place, but they wanted to have a drink beforehand and insisted she come.

A girl next to her blabbers, "There's a sexuality that we can only experience under the effects of alcohol. That's what drinking is: welcoming what otherwise remains hidden. Of our own desire. And sure, it's practical, not to know that about yourself. But drinking is to make a point of confessing, to shine a light in the dark."

She's a radiant redhead who must have known Claudine well and seems to adore her. Sometimes she puts her hand on Pauline's, or lets it linger on her thigh. She sends charming glances her way, smiles of great understanding. She speaks with her hands to the boy who's driving.

Pauline yawns, then sneezes loudly into her fingers. At the party, they kept passing around a CD with lines of coke on it. She tried it, her first time, without really knowing why. It didn't do anything to her except make her sneeze.

The redhead continues theorizing, "I would never have known that I liked to be fucked like a whore if I hadn't had sex while drunk. Sex with alcohol, it's not the same as sober sex, you accept yourself more. It's savage, actually."

She's the one who wanted Pauline to come with them: "We're not going without Claudine!" And Pauline followed, she was tired of the party. Now she has a headache.

Suddenly, she calls her as a witness. "Right? Claudine, you're not saying anything, what do you think?"

"I think you talk a lot. Other than that . . ."

She takes advantage of the other two laughing to keep quiet and be forgotten. The girl has other things to say. "The first time I had an orgasm, I was completely drunk.

And it wasn't a coincidence: alcohol opens up a girl's insides."

More laughter. Pauline snickers too, trying not to make waves. They all have this extremely casual way of talking about getting laid that turns every quip vulgar. She would have preferred they take her home. Maybe the bar isn't far and she'll be able to walk back.

But in fact it's not really a bar, more of a nightclub.

As soon as they arrive, one of her new friends—whose name she doesn't know but who knows hers because he knew Claudine and seems to like her—suggests that they go to the bathroom to "do some more."

She begins to feel that it's having an effect after all. Those little details that make an enormous difference.

When they come back to sit down again, the other two have disappeared.

Pauline asks, "Where are they?"

He squints a little, like a psychic, replies, "They must have met up with their knitting club."

Then he bursts into laughter, she senses she should follow suit and laughs with him.

They stay there without saying anything. There is almost no one in the club and the music is fucking terrible. There must be other dance floors because people are coming and going nonstop. It's strange that people so worried about being "on trend" finish their nights in this kind of club. It feels a little like being in the middle of nowhere, in the eighties . . . It must be ironic. The guy stands up.

"I'm going to take a look around. Are you staying here?"

"I'll come with you."

It's not that she wants to move, but a guy had sat down

on her left, with his wife, and is staring intently. She's not going to stay there waiting for him to start chatting her up.

He goes down a little hallway; the other dance floors must be through there.

He stops on the landing, looks, continues, signaling for her to follow.

"Nothing's happening over there."

She follows closely behind him. He stops again, for a bit longer. She approaches to see what he's looking at.

When she masturbated for the very first time, she already knew the word and what it meant, but it took a few days for her to make the connection between that word and what she was doing.

Here, it's the same. She knows the term—sex club—and had an idea of what it meant. But it takes several minutes for her to understand where she is and what's going on.

At first glance, now that she's next to him, watching, it makes her think more of a hospice. Sick bodies, suffering and moaning, wretchedness approaching death, pale figures, deformed, searching for relief. Whispered groans from every direction.

It takes her a moment to understand that these people are fucking. At least, that sex is involved. Once you know, it's obvious. It's only bizarre at first glance.

Lurkers extend a hesitant hand, women arched and languishing without conviction. Gray, everywhere, no lights, no music. People move around slowly, snake their way through the bodies.

The place is like a war zone, just after a battle, when bodies are still writhing around, shouting for water when there's no one left to help them.

First, her eyes couldn't make anything out. But, little by little, they assemble the gestures and comprehend the details. It's not that they're having sex or enjoying themselves. It's a question of genitalia. In contact. Exhibited.

One girl at the edge of a bed. She's wearing a bodice, her breasts popped out a little. She's blowing a guy, staring up at him. He still has his shirt on, his pants down under his ass, which is flat and hairy. A badly aged fiftysomething man, flesh pale and flabby, round stomach, a sickly look, and the skinny thighs of an old man. He's bent over. He's barely hard, seems content. His cock is thin and slouched.

Around them, three men watch. Without doing anything, without saying anything. They're still in suits, just their dicks out, which they fiddle with half-heartedly. One of them starts to touch her breasts. Immediately she jerks him off, then turns her head and blows him in his turn, while continuing to stroke the other guy.

Seated next to them, another guy is being sucked off by an incredible girl, her back forms an impeccable triangle, she's on her knees between his legs, she blows him skillfully. He doesn't get hard at all. A couple watches them. The guy starts to get excited, really excited. He gets hard. But he doesn't dare get too close. He seeks the hand of his wife so she can take care of him. She's wearing a beige suit like people wear for communion. She shakes her head no, doesn't seem convinced that she's happy to be there. And even less that she's aroused. He insists, gently, firmly. He wants her to participate. He thinks that if his wife gets involved he'll be able to touch other people's wives.

Pauline watches him. She has a nephew just like him. The kid must be nine years old and he always wants people to play annoying games with him; he's really tiresome. But he doesn't let up, he wants people to play with him and will insist for hours. Snot-nosed brat and irritating as hell, some guys never grow out of it.

The girl on her knees has super long hair that goes down to her butt. She's overdoing it a bit, like: I'm the queen of blow jobs. The guy still isn't getting hard, but he plays with her head, her hair, her breasts. He keeps busy, legs spread.

Slow rhythms, from everywhere, muffled cries, sleazy moans. A very, very restrained bacchanal of meek and stubborn blasphemy. Underground.

A guy standing next to Pauline in the entryway stares at her for a good five minutes. A new arrival starts to do the same but even more insistently. So the first one makes up his mind, goes over to her, places a hand on her breast, a strange gesture, resolute but also vigilant: How is she going to react? He's still afraid of getting slapped, even here. She pushes him away and turns to leave. The second guy grabs her hand, gives her an imploring look. He reminds her of a hobo, really begging, he wants what he wants so badly you can tell he'd rob you at gunpoint.

Pauline whispers in his ear, "Let me go or I'll kill you."

In a very serious tone, not relaxed. He brings a finger to his temple, calls her a nutjob and backs away.

In front of the staircase, to her left, a tiny dark room. She recognizes the redheaded girl, standing, being eaten out by an old hunchbacked man kneeling between her thighs.

When she gets to the exit, the old blond woman who had kindly welcomed them informs her that she's sorry, but, "You may not leave alone."

"I can't do *what?*"

Stunned. She might just strangle the old woman, it's entirely plausible if things don't go her way. Now the alcohol is waning but she really feels the coke. She starts yelling immediately, waving her hands and threatening, "You give me my jacket and my bag immediately, I'm leaving right now and you have no right to keep me here!"

The old woman wants to know who she came with, pretty upset that someone raised their voice in her office, Pauline can't even tell her the name of the person she came with, she doesn't know this guy who seems to know her so well.

In the mayhem, he shows up, apologizes to everyone, leaves an outrageous tip, drags her by the arm.

Street, he's not angry, it actually made him laugh that she had such a fit; for once something unexpected happened. He offers to take her home. In the car, before starting the engine, he cuts two lines, offers her one.

"I had no idea coke made you so crazy."

"It's not the coke. If I want to leave, I'll do what I like. It's not jail, what's their problem?"

"You know the rules though. You should have told me you were over it . . . You got bored?"

"Yes."

He laughs, changes speed, drives like a show-off.

"That's the first time I've ever seen you stand around while we're out . . ."

Then he puts on some music, the song is nice; it transforms the whole scene.

The city is enormous and chic, full of lights and surreal people everywhere, wind through the window, cool.

It's like living on the big screen, leaning back in her seat.

Claudine used to go there with them, and she did things there. In that dreary atmosphere, her, so blond and spirited.

And she used to sleep with Sébastien. He did all kinds of things to her and in every hole, every position.

During the party, earlier, a man had cornered her and started talking about all the things they had done together, how he had fucked her in the ass and stuck a lamp up her vagina.

It's been exactly three months since she died. Pauline's not angry anymore; on the contrary, she's come to a certain understanding. Claudine is closer than ever, really.

Impossible for Pauline to understand why she did that, all that, with men. It's like impoverishing yourself, a failure of self-preservation. Gaining nothing, in fact, other than a heap of bad memories that you lug around like a lost soul.

The guy leaves her in front of her door. The street is still deserted, funny to see it like that. The sun is just starting to rise, she gets out of the car, he hands her a ball of bud that he just found in his pocket, kindly says goodbye. He must have really liked her sister.

On her floor, the door is kicked in, left slightly ajar. At first she's scared, she hesitates to enter. In case someone is waiting for Claudine, to subject her to who knows what.

Standing in front of her doorway, immobile. The latch has been torn off, the sight terrifies her, she imagines herself as the door for a few seconds. Antagonized, open, easily vanquished.

Then she understands. A leap in her chest at having guessed.

She goes in. Lying on the couch, Sébastien is asleep, fully dressed. The TV is still on. She goes to sit against his stomach, puts a hand on his arm, waits for him to wake up.

When he opens an eye she asks, "Come to bed?"

In the same tone in which she's asked him 150 times. And he follows her like he's done 150 times, groggy, rubbing his neck, as if they had parted ways the night before.

Sleeping against each other, she situates herself inside his skin, an old habit, right away she knows where to put his arm, there's nothing unfamiliar about him, he is her sleep. She sees nothing but him, the tip of his shoulder and neck close-up, around her there is nothing but his breath, his scent, and his skin, she is completely inside of him.

He says, "I lost it tonight, I had to see you."

His large body is honest, only wishes her well, she rediscovers that unique familiar intimacy. "I missed you so much."

Then, "We have to fix the door tomorrow."

So she pretends to sleep, her hand strokes his back, calms him. On the inside, she begs him, *Don't ever leave me alone, don't let me do what I did again: no matter what, don't ever leave me free to go see what it's like outside.* She thinks of the heroines in the stories she read when she was a little girl, who follow seemingly trustworthy wolves. It's as if she has returned from the woods: she risked something serious, that she comprehends only vaguely, but feels distinctly, hideous things that smile at her. *Don't ever let me go back there.*

And she trusts him, he'll know how to keep her in check, watch over her all the time, as he did in the past.

That morning, probably because she's hungover, she thinks again of Claudine, who had no one to sleep with, to wake up to, to behave for. No one next to her, concerned with shielding her from the worst.

"*IL FAIT CHAUD, il fait de plus en plus chaud . . .*"

All the windows wide open, the noises on the street sound like they're coming from inside. You'd think they lived on a terrace.

Pauline is on her stomach, nestled in the pillows, one leg extended, the other bent. She looks like a baboon, bare ass sticking out of her short blue satin nightdress.

Next to the bed are a shoe, a T-shirt rolled into a ball, an open book, and the wrapper of a Miko's ice cream bar.

Sébastien counts the cigarettes, glances at the time, speculates whether it's possible to hold out until tomorrow before going to buy more. He sighs.

"You don't want to run to the tabac? It would be good for you to get out a bit."

She doesn't even respond. He insists.

"I'm always the one who goes grocery shopping."

She laughs, slumps in the bed.

"That's what's good for me!"

She turns around and sits down, takes the tray with everything on it to roll another joint. She makes her list.

"You'll need to get bread too. What are we eating tonight?"

She thinks, scratches a mosquito bite.

"You should get tomatoes and ham."

The whole week passed like that, in peaceful bursts, nothing to do other than take showers, get out of bed to go lie on the couch in front of the TV, drink Coke with ice. Sébastien, bare chested, spends hours at the window, never gets bored of watching what's happening below.

And Pauline never gets tired of running her hand along his back, all its reliefs, his man's body, toward the shoulders, it's like caressing her happiness. A vein goes from his wrist to his neck, she could trace it with her fingers for hours, rest her cheek against his chest.

She can't get over it: so much warmth. Even though she had waited for him for so long, and thought of him every night, crying over all that absence, she had still forgotten just how much good it does her.

They didn't talk about it again. Except that he often kisses her in the corner of her eye or just behind the ear, very softly, he surrounds her with a thousand precautions, to be sure she doesn't need anything, and tells her a hundred times a day, "If I lost you, I'd go crazy."

He doesn't talk about prison either. When she asks he says, "It's in the past, I don't even think about it anymore." She tries to figure out how it's changed him, she finds nothing. He's the same, completely the same as before.

He listened to her story, the whole thing, asks questions about Nicolas. "I don't trust your sister's friends," in a knowing tone. She bursts out laughing, ready to tease him a little. He doesn't like when she broaches the subject, he asks her to continue, "So, after, what did you do?"

She tells him, the heels, the makeup. She leaves out the

men in the street. She tells him, Nicolas again, the lies he told her. And the nightmare of the other night, the party with those idiots. She leaves out the nightclub.

He takes her in his arms like he's comforting a child. "It's okay, it's over now."

And he's sad for an entire night after learning that Claudine is dead. But they don't say a word about it to each other. She leaves him in peace, hangs up the laundry, looks at the TV guide.

Leaves him the time to absorb the shock. Now that she has him all to herself.

He makes love to her like before, lying on top of her while kissing her, softly, cautiously.

She talks about the trip they could have taken, that she had dreamed about for so long. She wants to show him the pictures of places they could have seen. He very gently rebuffs her, "Baby, stop making yourself feel worse."

They watch TV, men doing a striptease. Sébastien is appalled by the spectacle. "They're so ridiculous!"

When he sees them in their G-strings, wriggling in every direction, he bursts into laughter. "Look at them! Seriously . . ."

Suddenly he asks, "It's not this ridiculous when girls do it. Right?"

As if it were obvious. Pauline shrugs her shoulders.

"What difference does it make?"

He gestures to the screen, the guys finish the number bare assed. She rubs her eyes.

"It's just a matter of getting used to it. In five years, it won't shock us anymore, we'll ogle nothing but the pretty chests of men."

The phone rings, Nicolas on the answering machine. She gets up and goes to answer it. Sébastien observes, "That guy calls every day."

Then recommends, "Make sure you tell him that I'm back. No need for him to hang around you anymore."

She takes it as a joke. He tells her that he's in the area, she suggests that he come by for a drink. Hangs up. Sébastien isn't crazy about the idea.

"You couldn't have told him to meet you in a café nearby? I'm not in the mood to see anyone."

She doesn't reply. He insists, "You can't call him back and cancel?"

"He was calling from a pay phone."

"He's that much of a loser that he doesn't even have a cell phone?"

"He's a loser in every way, actually. At this point, it's a lifestyle choice. I'm sure you'll think he's cool."

That thought vanishes as soon as Nicolas enters the living room.

What had been so natural—seeing him move around these walls—becomes embarrassing and bizarre. Each of his gestures that she had never noticed before strikes her as cumbersome and misplaced now that Sébastien is watching him.

Even though Sébastien remains silent, his disapproval puts a stop to everything.

Pauline ends up wondering what they had found to

say to each other when they hung out every day for months.

Almost right away, she can't wait for him to leave.

She's grateful that he realizes it; he doesn't stay long.

Grateful, also, that he leaves as if nothing had happened, without trying to ask her questions. Letting her pretend that everything is normal.

Once the door is closed behind him, Sébastien loses it.

"I don't think I've ever seen such a pathetic little fag."

"He doesn't show off, but that doesn't make him a fag."

"He's so puny, it would make people laugh if he tried to show off. You saw him, right? All shriveled and emaciated, he looks like a grandma."

She waits for him to get over it. Ends up laughing along with him. Won over by his bluntness. That cruelty that she likes about him, that makes her want to be his woman.

Later, full moon, Pauline watches him sleep.

It left a bad taste in her mouth, to see Nicolas and be totally incapable of defending what they had between them, simply because Sébastien was there and she was afraid of upsetting him.

Memories of her mother come back, from when their father would hit Claudine. She would beg him to stop, she would cry. But she would let him do it. He was a force you couldn't even try to restrain, that you just had to endure. The anger of their father was intimately connected to his presence. One didn't exist without the other. No man without his violence.

Pauline wasn't the one who got beat up, but she remembers it clearly. Huddled on the floor, forced against a wall, a ridiculously frail body, two arms crossed over her head. He is a sky unto himself, unleashed in a storm, and his voice thunders and rumbles. A disgruntled god. It's not the blows that hurt the most—that's just the punishment, for displeasing him so greatly. It's that black adult rage, nowhere inside of you to protect yourself.

Their mother, while this was going on, would sometimes find the courage to hold back a raised fist, stop it from striking too hard. And when their father would back off she would lean over the little girl, "See what you make him do?" Because the anger of a man is legitimate, one must avoid provoking it.

Next to her, Sébastien breathes deeply. Sometimes he places a hand on her, as reassuring as it is heavy.

Of course, it's her fear of him, too, that attaches her to him so plainly. If she's afraid, it's because he's a man.

HE'S JUST COME back from buying groceries, puts what he bought in the refrigerator. The telephone rings, it makes him angry, he shouts "Again!" while slamming the refrigerator door.

She picks up, so that he won't have to hear the three rings until the answering machine.

It's the big boss on the phone, "the velvet voice." The nickname suits him. He listened to their demo. He thinks it's intriguing, really, even exceptional, can they have dinner together, one night this week, before he leaves on vacation?

They agree on a date and she hangs up.

Sébastien asks, "Who was it?" She replies, "A friend," sitting down next to him. She doesn't really know if she'll go. But she doesn't know what to make up as an excuse in the event she does decide to meet him.

Before, she never lied to him. To be fair, before, she never did anything.

IT'S A RIDICULOUS restaurant, in the same league as the party. Flaunted luxury, nice lighting, a lot of silverware, waiters who refill their glasses before they're empty. So Pauline gets drunk quickly.

The big boss pulls out all the stops, acting like he really wants to take care of her. He garnishes his speech with "you, the artist." It's less to flatter her than to feed his own fantasy: to be surrounded by artists and play the patron.

He devours her with his eyes, dishes out compliment after compliment.

She lied to Sébastien, made up a good friend she met in Paris who really wants to see her.

She's really bored. Like a child during the grown-ups' dinner who isn't allowed to go play.

He's enthusiastic, brimming with joy.

"Your voice is remarkable. Have you taken lessons?"

"I went to a conservatory."

"I thought so. You have a gift, a gift that's been honed, you can tell right away . . . I was very angry with Martin for not recognizing your talent. I had a word with him, but

I'm not under any delusions, if I want something done well I have to do it myself."

He raises his glass, she meets his gaze as though diving into freezing water, clinks her glass. Then she gives him a big smile. She doesn't like him, not his greasy affability or his stupid self-satisfaction, even less his crass elegance. She looks around her, everyone there is sophisticated, jazz playing in the background. She looks at the women: Are they wearing corsets underneath so that later they can go blow old dudes in sex clubs? It seems all the men are old, a little rigid, they look deprived of air.

The big boss wants to make the record. She has no idea why she stays seated opposite him smiling like a dope instead of draining her glass, asking for her coat, and taking off.

Actually, it's pretty straightforward. She wants to take a big trip. She wants to make a few bucks and have a legitimate vacation.

He's paternal with her, very bossy.

"We'll have to find you a songwriter."

"I like to write my own lyrics."

He snickers, amused.

"I know. But there are people, it's their job . . . I'll introduce you to someone."

She pushes back.

"I think my songs are good the way they are."

"A rebel, huh?"

As if it were a good joke, something that would pass quickly. He's all tender, nevertheless he adds, "It worked in the eighties, the whole raised-fist, fuck-the-system, long-live-anarchy thing. But that doesn't work anymore, these days."

She eats what's on her plate without responding. A terrible salad, not even fresh, pretentiously presented.

He has opinions about everything, categorically. She imagines him, every morning, standing by the window of his suburban house in Neuilly, hands on his hips, chin raised, deciding, "Okay, so now it's like this, like this, and like this."

He's more cautious about the other thing he has to say. "You have a big sound problem. Who did the production?"

"Nicolas, a friend. He borrowed the equipment, it didn't really work."

"I'm rather afraid that it's not just the equipment. He's your boyfriend?"

"No, he's only a friend."

He's relieved, visibly. That must have been the only black spot on the image: if she's sleeping with this guy, it'd be tough to lose him. But if they're just friends, he's not a problem. The concept of friends for him must have been relegated to school, the people you play some soccer with. After that, things must have taken a more serious turn: the others, all those rivals to eliminate.

When the waiters come to take away her plate, he keeps talking, he doesn't even see them. It's effortless, it's natural: there are people around who gravitate and serve him.

He asks, he is already pained for her, he has some difficult news to break, "And you're very attached to him, this Nicolas?"

"Very. If I'm with you here today, it's thanks to him from start to finish."

He sighs, there are things she has to learn.

"It might be thanks to him that you're here. But he certainly won't take you much further."

"His beats are good."

She doesn't think about it for a second. She knows very well that they're crap, muddled, unbalanced, and unexciting. But the big boss refuses to hear it. It's clear that he understands zilch, he acts like a music lover but he's mainly a big mafioso. All that interests him is putting his people to work, so that it all stays in the inner circle. He wants to bring her into his machine, with the others, to feed it.

He leans toward her, tries to be convincing.

"You have everything it takes to become a big star. And I'm prepared to do everything to help you. You have to understand: we don't get to the top in a group, we go alone, and those who stay behind stay behind, that's how it is."

She searches for the words.

"I need him, for a whole bunch of reasons. I need him for this album."

The boss shakes his head no, really sorry he has to teach her how hard life is.

"You don't need anyone. Emotion is emotion and business is business. You shouldn't be afraid of working with better people, and I am going to introduce you to them."

She acquiesces, she swallows it. She thinks: it's their first meeting, she'll wear him down, she won't let up on anything.

He gets on her nerves with his clichés. She wants to ask him: And what is your life like, for you to talk this way?

End of the meal, the big boss gets to the real question, his eyes narrow and lewd, all professional pretense gone.

"Do you go out often?"

She shakes her head no. He's chock-full of complicity.

"Friends have told me . . . Very close friends, good people, it wasn't to gossip or . . . anyway, I learned that you frequent . . ." He fumbles for the right words. She puts out her cigarette, lets him struggle. He finds the term: ". . . swingers clubs."

She nods. He explains that sometimes he also . . . in the same tone he might use to say, "I, too, plant bombs sometimes."

So it was that, from the start. He calls to the waiter passing by, takes out a credit card from his wallet, hesitates, puts it back, takes out another. She asks for another whiskey, he frowns a bit but orders it. Then she waits for him to suggest that they go there together, just to have a look around.

She remembers, in one of the pamphlets she took from the travel agency, how white the sand is on those beaches. She would do anything to plop her ass down on it.

AUTUMN

PAULINE WALKS OUT OF THE METRO. THE WHITE light leaves things gray and cold. Flower market nearby, display bursting with colors that seem out of place. A skater glides by, sort of grunge but also kind of clean cut. She passes an unbelievable woman who looks like a panther, tall boots thin legs white leather vest, like she's from another era. As she passes, the woman gives her a little smile.

A slight headache, from the accumulated drunken nights, it won't pass until after the first sip of wine.

Waiting to cross, she feels the cold along her arms.

Now she's used to it, looks scrutinizing her as she walks by. She doesn't even pay attention to them anymore, would be surprised if tomorrow she passed by unnoticed.

Photo shoot. Low-budget studio at the end of a shitty courtyard.

The photographer has a cold, isn't feeling great. He examined her like an expert when she introduced herself. In ten seconds he'd decided on the best look for her, gave instructions to the makeup artist and to the stylist. Without even turning toward Pauline—"What do you think?"—he takes care of everything. He's found some getup for her to squeeze into. Now just have to get rid of everything that doesn't match.

Pauline stays seated for a long time on an uncomfortable chair while a young girl paints her entire face with foundation. She doesn't think about Pauline, talks with her colleague.

So Pauline learns unintentionally that they're very badly paid, it's starting to get ridiculous, that the guy does coke, when he doesn't have any it's hell on earth, and that someone presented a lame collection the other night.

Then she's in the hands of the stylist, Pauline tells her that she doesn't want to wear the shoes because they're ugly and way too small. The stylist rolls her eyes.

Then she's standing in front of him. At first he's unpleasant.

"They told me you knew what to do in front of the camera. Supposedly you make Marilyn look clumsy by comparison. So make an effort, shit."

At this point she feels so incapable of staying in that absurd light any longer that she decides to tell him to fuck off.

But they're interrupted.

A visitor for the photographer. Ten minutes vanish. And he comes back all reinvigorated, rubs his hands together, puts on music. He tells her, "Dance, just to see," and it's true that she can really move.

Then he gets heated, circles around her.

"Show me your eyes now, show me."

And gives orders that she executes, he pummels her with compliments, "Yes, that's good, just like that."

Then it's over, he distractedly shakes her hand. She finds herself outside again. Her stomach is wrecked. Humiliation, she wants to vomit. She ended up doing exactly what he wanted her to do. Why didn't she leave? During the shoot, she felt like she was tapping into her inner self, even that it excited her, in a filthy and totally overwhelming way, to enter into that game.

Gestures came to her that she had never done before. Demeanor of a lascivious woman that she belittled herself to imitate. It was enough to hear him prompt, "Keep going, yes, like that," and to feel him walk around her for her to flaunt herself like a whore. As if it were second nature.

The massive hostility it used to provoke in her, to see a girl "lacking self-respect." Things were so clear back then: what everyone does, they decide. She was still unaware of how easy it is to get carried away.

She had isolated herself to such an extent that she had never crossed paths with any false guides, any silver tongues.

Now that she has stepped outside, she feels like everything is slipping away from her.

She thinks of Claudine often. Her aversions change with time.

In junior high Claudine became a woman overnight. A transformation as rapid as it was radical. Welcomed from all sides with applause.

Claudine, who until then had only accumulated abuse and was of no interest to anyone, had become "a beautiful young woman." That was enough for people to accept her. And she had quickly understood that it would be enough for people to adore her.

She who had taken up the habit of always slumping in her chair, keeping as low a profile as possible, had suddenly landed a fantastic deal: act like a girl, then you'll be able to stand up straight.

She took it as gospel, devoted herself to it entirely.

Pauline observed the metamorphosis and its accompanying celebration as though she were witnessing reality derailing itself. Stupefied, at first she had hoped that all these people would wake up and act reasonable again. But they revealed themselves to be unanimous and inflexible: encouragement from all sides.

As a response, Pauline became the only surviving witness of their young childhood. She never missed an opportunity to remind Claudine of what she had been, what she should never forget being. Slow, dim-witted, awkward. An idiot. To a pitiful degree. An idiot to the bone.

Claudine did the same to her, seizing every opportunity to reduce her sister to what she was: unattractive, unlikable, ugly and drab, not even nice.

SHE KNOWS THE path by heart, to get to the record label. She has to go over there all the time—see this, take care of that, meet so-and-so, sign things.

The receptionist is always friendly with her. Takes her for an idiot, like everyone else. No one tries to talk to her, they're all already up to speed: she's hot as hell, but she's not all there.

It was disconcerting at first, catching eyes rolling every time she said anything, and the badly stifled giggles if she made a critique. All she had to do was open her mouth and people were lying in wait for the enormous idiocy that would inevitably come out. She couldn't even say, "I could really go for a coffee," without them making fun of her.

Frankly, the people at the label aren't exactly geniuses themselves.

Seated in Martin's office. He calls someone every time she's there, he says three words, it rings, he's on the phone for a full fifteen minutes, then three more words, it rings, and off he goes again for another fifteen minutes.

He is visibly angry with her. He does everything as he should because the boss is watching. But he does not appreciate that they forced her on him. She becomes his punching bag.

Today, he observes her in silence, pensive, then frowns.

"We'll have to get your nose redone."

"Great, I'll go tomorrow."

"I'm serious, Chloé is the one who told us. I'm going to look into it."

"Please, keep me posted."

They talk about her when she's not there. And when she shows up they hit her with "We'll have to . . ." and "Don't forget to . . ."

They're bursting with fantastic ideas, totally original. She finds them all laughable.

He's more bitter than usual because yesterday the boss got angry. She said yes to the songwriter, yes to the sound guy, yes to the stylist. They have what she wants: a lot of money. She's waiting for the day she can get her hands on it.

She didn't want them to replace Nicolas. She thought that in choosing a single point of resistance she could hold out. They can't stand working with someone who isn't already known. They've identified the talent, he's in their binder and they won't go looking elsewhere. It's a kind of reflex: the job has to revolve around a small number of people, otherwise the riches dry up.

So the boss summoned her, much more enraged than usual.

"Listen up, Claudine: if we don't make this record, I'll be very disappointed, but tomorrow when I wake up, I won't be devastated."

She was sitting in his office, the disgruntled boss was waiting for her to make the right decision. All of it is for her own good, so why is she being a pain in the ass?

She said that he was right. Back home, called Nicolas. She has to see him tonight.

She waits for Martin to finish explaining something to her, how it'll work in the studio. If it can be said in four or five sentences, it takes him seven or eight paragraphs. He is incapable of being concise.

Before she leaves, Martin signals that he's not finished.

"The boss wants to see you."

With a contemptuous sigh, to make it clear he knows why.

He can shove his contemptuous sigh up his ass. When she sits down opposite him, he loses his train of thought as soon as she shifts a leg.

She walks through the office. In the center, there's a huge room where people are busy working. Several lift their heads, pointedly, then gossip once she's gone.

Everyone knows why the boss wants to see her so often, that she was signed because he's screwing her.

She knocks before entering, but Martin had already called to let him know he was sending her over. When he speaks to the boss, he talks about her with respect.

Sometimes she finds an excuse. But she has to go, regularly, to the boss's office. He does the same things to her that Sébastien did to Claudine. As if they knew each other, or learned it from the same place. When the time comes, it's the same movements and the same words, even their faces resemble one another's.

It's a huge room, beautiful furniture, a small bar cart. His desk is immense, and sturdy. She lays her whole body on top of it with him on top of her.

"What's new?"

Each time, it plays out the same way. Fifteen minutes of discussion, he takes keen interest in the album, gives advice, orders, notes down things he can't forget to do for her. That he never forgets to do. He takes care of his new singer very well. He pours her a drink, shows concern for her smallest problems. He treats her like a queen; it's part of the show.

It's an image that he creates for women, a moral duty to be gallant with them. Because they are pure, beautiful, venerable. He's old school, from a time when women were truly distant, strange animals, deprived of everything except a man's pleasure.

So he showers them with attention. Otherwise, it wouldn't have the same relish when he enters their every hole, treating them like good little whores. He has to venerate them a little to be able to really debase them.

Short silence. And it begins.

"It's hot out. Why don't you open your blouse a bit?"

He watches her do it. He likes for it to be slow, button by button. Then she has to fondle her breasts, it can go on a good five minutes; the spectacle renders him speechless.

"Lean back a little, rub your chest, yes . . . Now take off your bra, so I can see your beautiful tits."

Then he starts with the funny noises. It's not a laugh, it's not a moan, it's his funny noise that he makes when something excites him.

She does what he says, each time it's disconcerting that just the act of her showing her body can rile him up so much.

It's that she does it for him, it's the shamelessness, or who knows what. In any event, it's really something.

"Spread your legs now, take off your panties, slide them down, there you go . . . Touch yourself in front of me, finger your pussy."

Then she has to moan a little. The idea that she is aroused goes right to his head. Every time it's like some big miracle, he's transcendent: a woman who orgasms, in front of him, with impunity, transports him to other realms.

When he takes out his little prick, all ugly but rigid despite his age, she's embarrassed for him. His measly red thing, it's a whole adventure for him, to see it screwing her, as if it were a saber.

"Come here, on your knees, get underneath the desk and make me happy."

It's funny how men don't have self-esteem issues. At least not until later. Every part of his body is gross, Mother Nature has not been kind to him, but he doesn't think he has anything to be embarrassed about, he only thinks of his own enormous pleasure. It must be nice, to be like that—terrible for anyone who has to put up with him, but pleasant for him. Only thinking of his own perspective, staring out at others, never thinking of the opposite.

Then he's doing her doggy style, she cries out the way he likes, he plows into her, saying, "I'm going to make you come."

And slapping her ass; when it's over it's all red.

He's convinced she likes it. Once, though, he asked her, "You're not faking it with me, are you?" She replied, "Why would I do that?" and that completely reassured him. He's crazy about his cock, he never gets over it, that he has one and that it gets hard. It's not difficult to convince him that it works well, pushes all the right buttons inside of her. He was already sure of it.

He thinks if she's capable of doing it with him, it has to be because she adores it too. He must think that prostitutes are born with a mark on their forehead that distinguishes them from other women. He must imagine that if she didn't like it, her hole would stay closed or her thighs would be completely welded together. It's that he believes a lot of bullshit, it's that he likes women, those splendid and different animals . . .

He said to her once, "There are people who have their doubts about us. They think you do it out of self-interest." He smiled, satisfied, wise to secrets unknown to others. "They have no idea what you're like."

And it's an enormous compliment. He thinks of her as carefree, liberated, precisely the kind of woman he likes.

If he knew the actual effect his nub of rotten meat has on her, he would surely think there was something wrong with her. Obviously out of the two of them, it must be her who has a problem.

Women are never as crazy as men are capable of being, eager to do it all the time with everyone in every way. Women, they have a hole, it always works, and they're there, with stomachs capable of blowing up and growing a child. They don't pass the time with their thingamajig worried, wondering if it can grow and go into ecstasies when it's hard.

When he feels it coming, he panics, he pulls out of her, tells her to turn over while he jerks off onto her breasts.

Once again trying to convince himself that something comes out of him. A pittance, a bit of white snot. They're all crazy about seeing it on something.

Then they put their clothes back on and talk for another minute. He is full of benevolent respect, listens to her, is interested in her, reassures her.

Before she leaves, he asks, each time, "You're sure you don't need anything?"

SÉBASTIEN IS SICK of being there, he repeats it every day. She tries to make him wait. She suggests that he take a vacation, but he sighs when she says that. "And with what money would you like me to do that?"

He thinks it stinks, in the street. As if it weren't safe to breathe. He thinks the people are unfriendly. That everything is expensive, he goes nuts every time he goes out for a coffee, the next day he brings it up again: "Fifteen francs! And in a shitty, disgusting local bar. I got one look at the john and came back to piss here." He thinks the neighborhood is unhealthy. "Fuck, it stinks of poverty. I already have enough of my own without having to deal with other people's."

Every day when she gets home, he's sitting in front of the TV.

It's still the same story, between them, with one difference: he's the one who stays at home, waiting for her to finish with her wheeling and dealing.

She tries to find things to distract him. Obviously without money, it's not easy. "You don't want to go to a museum? Apparently there are free days." "That's it, yeah. I'll go take knitting classes while I'm at it, I'll have a ball."

Every day when she gets home, he hides: the housing assistance office worries him. Same with the people from income support—they refuse to believe that they're not a couple. As if it were her fault: "They said they'd do an inspection." "We'll say you sleep on the couch, why not?" "Why not, that's it, take them for idiots."

And she says, "You don't realize it now, but it'll be okay, this album will come out and it'll work, then we'll leave. Do you want me to show you where we'll go?"

All the leaflets she had put aside, it was for the sole purpose of being able to show him. He doesn't want to hear it. "You're a singer like I'm a plumber, I don't get why you bore me with all that."

He flips through a few magazines, opens one to a photograph of a girl with long legs, shoves it in her face: "Is this what you want? Is that it? To show your ass to everybody? Is that what gets you off?"

When he's in that mood, she laughs, goes to look for a porno magazine; Claudine has plenty in her apartment. And she shows him one of the photos, facial or fellatio, she says, "My ambition, you see, is to one day be able to do that," in her best skank voice. He doesn't want to laugh at first, but she keeps going for as long as it takes. Until he wants to join in on the game, calms down, changes his mood.

She almost never talks about the album. Just keeps him up to date, the bare minimum. She can tell it annoys him more than anything. "But you're too old to be a singer." "But darling, I'm twenty-five . . . That's not old."

He isn't even two years older than her, he already sees himself at his worst. It changed him, his year locked up. Little things about him that she didn't pick up on at first, but that have become more acute over time. As if the walls had closed in on him to the point of smothering him completely, he's overflowing with a desperate rage.

She feels sorry for him. Convinced that he's wrong, that the sun will shine for them one day too, and even soon. When they're on vacation, far away from here, he'll gradually return to the way he was before. His sense of humor, his voracious desire.

Apart from her and the big boss, no one believes in the album. That she'll really kill it. She never says it out loud. But she knows it, irreproachably. It will change everything, everything they know now will be over. And he'll see, he who thinks that everything is lost and that they'll be in the red forever.

They're going to hit the big time.

And knowing that, day after day, she tries to give him what she can, so that he holds on until they reach the other side.

Fortunately there's the TV, to sit in front of instead of talking to each other.

She bought groceries. He opens the second bottle, she's drunk, ends up letting herself go.

"They're a pain in the ass about everything, you know, the lyrics, my outfits, the production . . ."

She knows it irritates him when she talks about the

album. Why can't he think of it with some detachment, take it like a kind of experiment? That night, she lets loose.

"I'm afraid of them, seriously. It's not so much that they're mean, it's a question of culture, I think, of experience. They've been surrounded by the music industry since they were little, they can't imagine anything else."

And since he doesn't say anything, and she's getting really plastered, the words come out more easily. She tries to explain it better. She still has this fantasy, it's almost a cliché, that he will help her, understand her.

She continues, openly bitter, "It's a funny feeling, to be taken for an idiot. Because for them my boobs are too big, my lips are too big, my eyes are too big, my hair is too blond. You can't imagine how much they despise me."

It's the first time that she's talked to him about this. He doesn't turn to face her, looks at her out of the corner of his eye, severely.

"I don't understand why you're complaining. You got what you wanted, didn't you?"

It's sad. That he speaks to her this way. That he doesn't put his head on her lap, tell her that they're all jerks, that she shouldn't give a damn about them, that she's great, that he cares about her.

PLACE D'ITALIE. NICOLAS is waiting for her. He finished his beer a while ago. He doesn't have anything to pay for it, he speculates about her arrival, isn't sure whether to have a second.

Since her boor of a boyfriend started living with her,

Pauline always meets up with him outside of the apartment. He's a big hulking man, the kind who beat up four-eyed nerds during recess, the kind girls often like. In his presence, next to him, she erases herself, a way of withdrawing. Bridled like that, she's less fun.

It was when he saw her with him that Nicolas first got the idea that he wanted to fuck her.

Since then, as soon as she turns up, he gets hard. He has to be mindful of what pants he wears, has to go to the can regularly to ease the pressure.

When he looks at her, he doesn't even see Claudine anymore, gone is the fear of causing pain, the silent pact they sealed.

White skirt suit, blond bun. Unintentionally the perfect high-class whore. Confident walk, as if she were strutting in sneakers. With her boyfriend back, she keeps her distance. But it passes after two or three drinks.

She talks to him about the album a lot. Takes everything really personally, reacts negatively to everything immediately, takes offense at every little thing. Whatever her motives, he really likes to feel her anger. It's what gives him the biggest hard-on. While she's furious and swearing like only she can do, he imagines her, stammering, reared up underneath him, clinging tightly to his back.

He listens to her, getting even harder. Tonight, she is more ferocious than ever. A soul black as coal with a glowing red center. Hands clenched in a fist beneath her chin, she looks like she's praying, eyes lowered, while delivering her tirade:

"Is there a word for misogynist or chauvinist but the other way around? Fuck, I hate men, I wish I had the words to really express that."

But it's the inevitability that really gets him going. She wants it as bad as he does, it would be enough for him to get close to her for her to realize it. He's going to fuck her like a madman. Everything happens between her thighs, she has to let him get in there because it would be so fucking good for both of them. She'll press her pelvis to his while tightly squeezing her legs, knotted around his waist.

He observes her, the top of her thighs, crossed. And her way of getting red with rage when some guy passes by and looks at her. Always on display against her will. It makes him want to tie her up, do two or three nasty things to her, as if up till now it would have been ridiculous to do so with another girl. He barely needs to respond to her, she's getting carried away all on her own.

"You'd think they'd get over it, that obsession of seven- or eight-year-olds with the 'honk honk' boob-grabbing thing, but nope, fifty years later men are still just as stupid as they were when they were kids."

It's become a fixed idea for her, discourse promising all males a single and violent punishment. It's even worse when she talks to him about it, it makes him want to slide inside of her, to see if there's a way to make her moan and squirm. There's plenty of trash he dreams of whispering in her ear. Specifically to her, because he's convinced that she's never wanted to orgasm from that kind of thing.

She is devastated by the immensity of the problem.

"It's undeniable, the masculine sex is a subspecies. And they're crazy about their cocks, crazy because of them. It's not even girls who excite them, it's the idea that they'll have a boner. They can't get over it, but we're not all going to stay hung up on it for fifteen thousand years. It's their problem, and they can figure it out . . ."

Relieved, it's been a good hour now that she's been ranting, she empties her glass and apologizes, smiling, "I haven't given you much of a chance to talk. How are you?"

"I want to fuck you, badly."

It had to come out.

She is flabbergasted. Tries to take it as a joke.

"Clearly you're listening to me very attentively."

"That's irrelevant. We need to fuck."

She gives him a dirty look and changes the subject. He gives her a break until they finish their drinks, acting as if nothing had happened.

While she's paying the bill, he gets back to it.

"You stayed here with me because you know perfectly well that we're going to do it."

She turns somber, stares at her hands.

"I would have preferred not to know."

He took her into an alley.

They fucked on the ground, maintaining the intimate conviction that they were rolling in sand, on the edge of the sea. Anyone could have come upon them but they weren't interrupted. They took their time, before and after and between each round.

At first she pushed him off when he tried to go down on her, as if it were something unclean. But then she let him do it. It was like his mouth knew her pussy better than she did, knew how to love it and touch it in all the right places, his tongue precise and soft.

He buried himself in her slit, pounding her with his cock, no hands, striking until he hit bottom.

He put a flower in her gut, with a beating heart and

petals blossoming in all directions. Long, soft, and smooth. He put a sea in her insides, rocked by his rhythms.

He talked about her nice ass, how warm she was inside, how he filled up her pussy and how much she loved it.

She was surprised to orgasm, at how long it takes, all the build-up and the explosion, so white.

Surprised, but more astonished at not having sought it out earlier, to have only managed it that night.

Then they were on the sidewalk. A bit distant all of a sudden, not really knowing how to act around each other anymore. She looked at the time on a parking meter. Crash-landing back to reality: Sébastien, who she needed to get back to and whom she had cheated on once again.

At the taxi stand, Nicolas's body sought hers to say good-bye, already seemed misplaced.

She went home without making a sound. Sébastien was sleeping. Took a shower. And lying next to him, intense regret for what she had done.

From that moment on, she eliminated Nicolas from her thoughts. He calls a few days later, his voice has become menacing. She waits for him to forget her.

One night, she comes back from the record label, a bit late, the big boss wanted to talk. His latest obsession is anal. He had bought a tube of lubricant. She refused, knowing that she wouldn't be able to say no for long.

Sébastien is in front of the TV. She walks around the

living room, lightly cheerful. Then she stretches, saying, "I'm going to take a shower, it'll do me some good."

"If it's so I won't know, there's no need . . . You smell like sex from ten feet away, like you do every time you come back from there."

He's not any angrier than if he had said: you forgot the bread again. He didn't even make it into a big deal.

The scent of entangled limbs. Not her own, nor someone else's, that very particular fragrance created when people have rubbed up against each other.

She searches as fast as possible for something to say to defend herself, to fix it. And thinks, she's a complete idiot—several months she's been lying, and he's watched her do it.

He keeps changing the channels for several minutes, his face a mask. This kind of hostility is much worse than getting angry or asking her for an explanation. It's already too late, he doesn't care anymore. A slight annoyance, an irritation.

She stays standing, planted there like a dope. The shame burns in her heart.

How long has he known, said nothing, let her lie.

She would've like to sit down next to him, own up to it, confess, relieve herself of the weight, beg him to understand.

But there's the smell, she can't go near him.

Finally he adds, without even turning his head, "On second thought, go clean yourself up. Otherwise I'll vomit."

His impeccable profile, *You are everything that I love, you are everything that counts, look at me, at least give me your anger, at least give me something, there's still a connection, there will always be a connection, at least show it to me.*

Shower. Soap all over her, she scrubs, like she does every time. Even washes her hair and shines her nails, hostile and maniacal gestures, scouring her whole body. She cries beneath the water, stays shut in there for a long time, afraid to leave.

I want for you to understand, for you to still love me, for you to protect me from all of that, for you to protect me from myself, for you to stop me from doing it, for you to understand how sad it is, to be capable of doing that, to open yourself like I did, to someone other than you, the times he made me orgasm, I would have preferred not to know what I really am.

The towel is very dry, pretty soft, it smells good. She dries herself carefully, she's crying less. She'll explain it to him as best she can. She'll leave the bathroom, find the words one by one for him to hear what she has to say.

Now she is almost at ease. She can't do it anymore. She'll go see the big boss and announce: these games are over, I almost wrecked everything.

She must have stayed locked in the bathroom for a long time. When she comes out, the first thing she sees is that his things are missing from all over. He didn't have a lot, but a notebook always placed here, a few T-shirts piled there, an old book he drags everywhere. A few objects, not much, the void they leave jumps out at her as soon as she walks into the living room. She goes to look in the bedroom; he had enough time to pack his bag. Continues not to look at her. He gently pushes her aside to go into the bathroom, takes his shaving cream, his razor, his cologne, and his comb.

"What are you doing?"

As if it weren't obvious, as if there were a chance of

hearing him respond: "I'm doing a big clean-out," or "I'm putting away my summer clothes," or "Come on we're going on vacation, hurry up and pack your bags."

He presses his things down to be able to close his bag. He explains, "If I had wanted to be with Claudine, I would have gone to her."

"You did come to see her though."

"If you want me to pass by from time to time for a quickie, some coffee, and then take off again, that's not a problem, I can arrange it."

The tears come back, still noiseless, she feels them hot against her cheeks and dripping under her chin. He insists, "You have to tell me. Now that you've become someone I don't know, you have to tell me what you want, I can't guess."

"Why are you saying that I've changed so much?"

"And on top of everything you're fucking with me?"

For an instant, he gets a little angry, it's less cruel than the rest, but it hardly lasts. He just adds, "A year ago, when I went to jail, I was going out with a hell of a girl, a real lady. You never cheated on me, I'm sure of it, you never treated me disrespectfully, you never demeaned yourself. I was proud of you, as soon as I saw some bitch on the street I thought of you, I was so fucking proud. But now, look at yourself, look at how you're dressed, look at how you walk . . . And who's boning you, over there? Is it a bunch of guys? Do you like it when they fuck you? Do you like it better than when it's with me? Is it good, do they screw you how you like? I respect you too much, you don't respect yourself at all anymore. There's nothing left of this relationship."

She doesn't have time to protest, he's put on his

jacket, he's already at the door. He turns back toward her, strokes her cheek. "I loved you so much. But now you repulse me."

She hears herself scream, fall to her knees, convulsions. One last time she sees his eyes on her, sees nothing in them but contempt mixed, even so, with a little pity. He slams the door behind him, she's lying on her back, she stamps her feet and tenses up, howls like a madwoman. She asks herself what kind of show she's putting on.

SHE WAKES UP for no reason, right in the middle of a dream, the sun has barely risen, the bed empty next to her, it takes her a few seconds to remember the night before.

No way of knowing from where she gets such an incredible tolerance for pain and heartbreak. Probably no greater than anyone else's, but it feels more intense because it's happening to her right now.

Waves of disgust churn inside her, lies, violent poisons. She sees herself in the big office, playing his games and doing things, it's impossible that Sébastien abandoned her for that. Just as it's unthinkable that he believes she's changed because of some lipstick and a few low-cut dresses. A misunderstanding, he'll come back. She can't lose him, it wouldn't make any sense, and no girl, anywhere, is made for him the way she is made for him, a misunderstanding, he'll come back.

She knows very well that that isn't true. She doesn't want to know.

Down below men are arguing, drunk, others try to calm them down.

The look he had, before, when he left. And she was on the ground, thrashing about like she'd lost her mind. Even though she knows that it sickens him.

She had never done it before.

Those were Claudine's games, tantrums at the first sign of a fight, and Pauline had watched her do it with disgust and exasperation.

Did it hurt Claudine as much as it hurt her when earlier . . . ? Did she, too, feel powerless, seeing herself shatter into a thousand pieces, no longer knowing what to do and so afraid of being written off as crazy?

Her only sister. Did it chill her in the same way, in the hands of men, seeing them go crazy just from watching her undress, did it chill her in the same way, to be carried away by desires as powerful as they are degrading?

Her only sister. Did she wake up in the same way, in the same bed, sun not yet up? There are tons of sleeping pills in the cupboard, next to the bottles of perfume.

Pauline gets up and gulps down two. Then she waits, lying down, crushed and nauseous. When you hurt the man you love, by tearing yourself down, diminishing yourself, there's a certain look he gives you. Then that gaze follows you everywhere, is sorry to see what it sees. It hurts down to the bone, not being who you're supposed be.

WINTER

THE MAKEUP ARTIST IS CURT. SHE IS ANGRY WITH her colleagues, who don't do a fucking thing and who hide instead of working. Tilts Pauline's head like this and turns her head like that, look up, now close your eyes. She had sighed when Pauline sat down. "It's going to take a while to do your foundation."

There are five of them getting their makeup done at the same time, lined up in front of a big mirror. The weather girl comes to kill time every so often, in a great mood.

Hairdresser. "What am I doing for you?" Just straightening. She tells her to use sweet almond oil on the ends, it's good for the hair.

Pauline hears that jerk Martin at the other end of the hallway, then he walks in, shrieking, "My darling! How beautiful you are!"

The first single hit two hundred thousand. In less than two months. He can hardly believe it. But it's made him very friendly, and even decently respectful. He defends her when she's attacked: "Okay, she got on her knees to get signed. But if you think that all it takes to blow up like she did is to give a little head . . ." with his affected airs.

He kneads her shoulders, asks her if everything's okay. She smiles all the time now. It's honestly become a kind of reflex; as soon as she hears noise, smile.

Dressing room. Flowers, alcohol, chocolates. Martin came with the publicist. The same person who had once asked, "Shall I send Madame Skank's single around to all the local kindergartens? Have to get to them early if you want to sell them that shit."

Two hundred thousand in your face, cunt. At least that's a language they all understand.

She's there to promote her second single. The producer is cool, seems nice. He tells people that she's a "good girl." He comes to see her. "Everything okay, need anything?"

She says, "I forget where the bathroom is."

He takes her. A line on the toilet bowl. She tries not to sniff too loudly.

The stage lights up, she does the show. She doesn't get along with the sound guy, the one who replaced Nicolas. He sulks at having to work with her because his friends make fun of him: "You're doing pop music for sluts now?" But he doesn't turn his nose up at the money. Sometimes, though, he changes a part without telling her, just to see how she reacts. Nice try, sweetheart, you can change the entire song, I'll figure it out, every time. She can easily make herself cry tears of rage by the second verse, and start belting enormous, disconcerting sounds. She's got this.

In the dressing room, everyone congratulates her. She takes flowers, declines Martin's invitation—"We'll go out for a drink, all together?"—to talk shit about everyone, who's gotten fat, who sells how much, who aged overnight, and who signed where.

A car brings her back to her place. The driver is an old

man, Spanish accent. He tells her how he left his wife fifteen years ago, on a whim, for a younger girl. And how he regrets it. "After six months, I understood what a mistake I had made." But she already had someone new. And since then, he's been waiting for her. "My children tell me I'm crazy. But I know that she's the one, there's no one else."

That's the main problem with coke, when you come down from it, it feels shitty. She could cry. She asks him, "And you think she'll come back?" He's sure of it. "I'm waiting for her. I've put some money aside, for us to grow old together."

Later, at home, a host of messages have accumulated on the answering machine. Newspaper reporters, TV producers, photographers from somewhere, radio hosts, and a bit of whoever asking for a bit of whatever. She listens to them, wonders if Sébastien will return her call. He went back home, he lives there with a cool girl she knows well. He did it so quickly. Just a matter of convenience.

The big boss left his congratulations, some "my sweetie pie," some "and I know that it's just the beginning," with some "I'm overcome with emotion."

The day after Sébastien left, she called the big boss. "Can we see each other?" "Yes, yes, of course, come when you like."

She arrived at the office. "I came to tell you that I can't make this album."

At first he thought she was scared; it was three days before the recording session. He took it lightly, patted her shoulder. "It's the big leap, huh? Now that you're here you want to backpedal . . . It's nothing. I believe in you. The day of, you'll be there, and you'll be incredible. You're made for this, I know it."

She shook her head no, unable to speak, still really mixed up. She started to cry, he approached her, she pushed him away with both hands, "Don't touch me anymore you fucking pig! Understand? I don't want to make your stupid album or keep playing your games!"

Then he behaved differently. He waited for her to calm down, canceled all his meetings, let his wife know that he would be home late. They stayed in his office until everyone had left. The first hours, she couldn't speak anymore, she wanted to leave but had to stop crying first, to avoid bursting into sobs in front of those people and making them laugh. It obsessed her, those people, she kept repeating, "And they'll be so satisfied, to know I got screwed."

The big boss let her voice her incoherent thoughts in her fucked-up state. "It's because of this album that he left. That's why I don't want to do it anymore. I don't want to be a bad person, can you understand that?"

And while she was unloading, she was regretting doing it in front of him, though it was definitely him that she had come to see. She was even angrier with herself because of that. "She passed on all her vice to me. I know I wasn't like this before. She passed on all this chaos, but I'm not her, I don't want this."

He figured it out on his own. He said, "I didn't know you had a boyfriend."

"That's none of your business."

Finally, he came to sit next to her. Before approaching, he raised his hand. "Don't worry, I won't touch you, I didn't know you were seeing someone." And suddenly, he started acting like he was talking to his daughter. He apologized, sincerely ashamed. "I think I was wrong about you, Claudine. You know, it's difficult to know things about someone if they never say a word of what they're thinking. I'm happy you came to see me."

Then he took out the whiskey, clinked glasses with her. "To the album, which will be fantastic. And your boyfriend will come back, no one leaves a woman like you. To all the good things in store for you."

He never made her come by his office again, not even a suspicious gesture. He followed the recording closely, and the release, even doubling his zeal, to prove to her what kind of guy he was. The kind you can count on.

She's at home. Not tired. She tries to reach her dealer, but his voice mail is always full. She mainly just wants to see him, he's the only person she really likes right now. He's always smiling, recounting his impossible missions; when he's not trafficking metro passes it's contraband cigarettes or Hermès scarves brought back from exotic countries. "We pass the tollbooth, I see border control, I felt myself dissolve. I said to myself: you're done for." And then he gets away with it every time.

She doesn't turn on the TV because she sees herself on it too often. Impossible to get used to her own stupid face. It takes a lot of work to sell that shit. She is surrounded by herself. Never has she existed so little, no life, nothing. But she's everywhere. People have violent words for her, she's the bitch you love to hate.

She rolls a big joint with two papers, to kill off her brain cells, she does it every night now. Doesn't feel well enough to run around in circles not giving a shit.

"CLAUDINE, PICK UP, it's important."

Dead of night. She was in the middle of a dream full of leaks, the walls in her apartment were crumbling plank by plank, and the ceiling was decomposing. She needs some time, to emerge and then to understand. It's the big boss on the answering machine. She doesn't move. Can't she sleep in peace?

He insists, "Pick up, please."

She's heavy when she gets up, everything in her wants to be asleep, to be lying down, hearing nothing. The answering machine cuts off, he had been talking for too long. She looks at the clock, it's 6:30. He gets up every day at that time, to work out. An old man's body needs to be looked after. It rings again immediately, she picks up. He's annoyed.

"You should have warned me you had done that. We could have done something . . ."

"Hang on, hang on. That I did what?"

"You can't guess? It involves a certain videotape. They wrote a huge article about it. Tomorrow all of Paris will be talking about it and nothing else."

"I still don't understand."

She could have fallen asleep where she was standing. And now's the moment he speaks in riddles.

"Your porno, my dear. It was going to catch up with you one day or another, you should have known. Why didn't you say anything? A big company bought it, they're going to do a lot of publicity for it, it's going to be bad bad bad for us—"

"My porno!"

"Are you telling me you don't remember?"

"No, no, no, I do. Of course. You don't forget something like that."

182

"Do you have it at your place?"

"Uh . . . no. I didn't keep it."

"I'll have it sent to me. Let's meet later, at one? We have to see what we can do. I'll warn the lawyer, he'll be there. I'll—"

"Can you send a courier with a copy for me too? To refresh my memory."

When she hangs up, it makes her laugh. A nervous laugh, inappropriate. But at the same time, it's genuinely funny.

She goes back to bed. And dives back into her dream full of leaks. The floor has given way, the apartment is threatening to collapse, and the landlord doesn't want to do anything about it.

It's called *Luck Be Two Ladies*, Claudine being one of those ladies. She's pictured on the cover, blowing a guy.

Pauline is more awake when it arrives. She hesitates before watching it.

It begins, Claudine is at home. Her own apartment, where Pauline is at this moment.

She's in front of her Minitel, bare ass under a T-shirt, very serious look, she writes down a telephone number, hits END CONNECTION. Then she calls someone. "So, my darling scoundrel, are you going to make me come?" She gives her address and the code, then tells him she's waiting for him, that they're really going to have some fun.

We see her getting ready. She takes a shower, then puts on a garter belt. It's all filmed at her place. We see her in front of the mirror, trying on sexy underwear. Then she puts on makeup and perfume. Right when she's done, the doorbell rings. She goes to open it for the guy, he starts groping her immediately, says that he's lucky. "I found me one hell of a girl."

He brought a bottle of whiskey, he wants her to serve him on all fours, he strokes her ass while she's doing it, pleased, "You didn't put on any underwear, like I told you, that's nice, your pussy's soft, you're already wet, you slut." Then he wants her to suck him off, but without using her hands. That's important: no hands. While she does that, his cell phone rings, he picks up. He explains, "I'm in the middle of getting a blow job. Hang on, don't hang up." And he tells Claudine, "Lick my balls a little," then to his friend, "You want to come over? She's the kind of whore that can handle two."

Pauline is sitting in front of the TV. She doesn't think much. She made a genuine effort to panic: *Everyone will see this and think it's me.* In the end, it's not so bad. Especially since Claudine performs so convincingly.

She lets it play. Against all expectations, it reminds her of things from when they were kids, foolish memories that she never thinks of but that have remained intact.

Claudine was great at gymnastics. On the balance beam and the uneven bars, she used to do incredible things. They were little girls at the time. She would wear the school T-shirt, canary yellow. She was like a fairy, doing really complicated routines, the little girls staring at her. She always wore barrettes. Their mother didn't want for her to have long hair, it was too annoying to maintain. She would cry every time they brought her to the hairdresser. And insisted on wearing barrettes. When she mounted the balance beam, she held herself instinctively straight, like a great athlete. She still had the body of a child, flat chest and little legs, but she showed off like an adult. And she had the right to; in one go, she launched herself, turned in the air, back flip, landed again on her feet, impeccable form, as if she had just whistled a little tune.

The friend in question has arrived, they're all in the bedroom. True to their word, they put it in all her holes. When she orgasms, she's beautiful. Even if their words are ugly, even if they don't treat her well, even if they have disgusting faces. When she orgasms—and it's hard to believe that she's faking it—she is truly beautiful. Her face lights up, relaxes, her eyes look elsewhere, a sort of laugh, or else she's about to start crying. She is nicely framed; in moments, she attains something like happiness.

They had a dog, when they were kids. As soon as they were alone, Claudine would shut it in a room. She would wait behind the door until he cried before she opened it. Then, she would get angry, give him a nasty beating, she hit him so much the dog would wail. Then she would close the door again, threatening him if he made a sound. The puppy, terrorized, didn't protest anymore. So she would go console him, taking him in her arms, he would be trembling all over, and she would kiss him everywhere. "My poor darling."

She used to punish all her dolls. When they had gone too far, she would tear off an arm, lecturing them maliciously, "You see what we do to girls like you? You don't want to learn, huh?" Then she would tear off a leg, "You'll end up learning your lesson, you'll see."

After, she takes off with the two guys in a car. Pauline didn't follow where they'd said they were going. She looks elegant, in a black suit, even though she's naked underneath.

They arrive at a club. There are a lot of teenage girls dancing, naked beneath their dresses, which are quite short. Claudine goes onto the dance floor, courageously shakes her ass. That, she doesn't do so well. She has no idea how to move.

As soon as they were old enough to go to parties, her sister would only dance to slow songs. Pretty early on, she abandoned all activity not directly related to seducing boys. She didn't read, nor did she have friends, nor did she do gymnastics, or anything other than please. She did it so well, it would have seemed ludicrous, dull, to bother with anything else.

Certain boys among them never recovered. Wrote her unbelievable letters, sometimes several years after she had let them court her. She would look at the envelopes, recognize the handwriting, and throw them away immediately, overwhelmed. "Why is that guy so clingy?"

And on top of it all, it was a tiny little town, she was the jewel of the neighborhood.

Still on the dance floor, she starts to do things with a girl, shimmying right up next to her, sticking her boobs out toward hers. It's the tantalizing redhead. Pauline recognizes her immediately, tries to think of her name: Claire. The one who put her hand on hers and wanted her opinion on everything.

They go at it, in the middle of everyone, there's a big circle around them, people are touching themselves. Mostly men, a lot of them.

Claudine never had a girlfriend. She was suspicious of other girls, and the opposite was even worse. She would say that she didn't like them: "They're all bitches." She couldn't stand for another girl to be as pretty as her. Apart from very famous actresses, preferably dead ones. As if it negated her; she needed to believe that she was the only woman in the world. The only one capable of triggering that kind of excitement in men.

For several minutes, there's nothing very pornographic about it—they kiss and touch each other, caress and say words the viewer can't hear, words that make them laugh, they bite each other a little and stare at each other, eyes gleaming. Then they take off their clothes and finger each other, go crazy over each other's breasts.

The redhead must have thought Pauline was acting cold the other night, given what they've shared. She's even prettier than in real life, her body looks good on TV. Pale, long. A sorceress. She's also beautiful when she orgasms, it's even moving to see them do it opposite each other, they make each other come with their fingers, one against the other, they don't break eye contact, until their eyes close as they start convulsing.

What was she thinking while she was doing that? While she was doing that and just before and just after, too? Did she watch herself? Did she feel proud? Did someone tell her that she was beautiful, more than ever, within that surrender?

Did she remember how adamant she was as a little girl? "You should never sleep with a boy who hasn't asked you to marry him. Otherwise he won't respect you anymore. Even if you really, really want to. He has to wait and marry you. Otherwise no one will want you anymore." But that was before she got her start. Rapidly, she changed her tune. "To hold on to a guy, you have to tell him he has a big cock and that he made you come like no one else has. You have to scream in his ears, not be afraid. Even if you're bored. Have to scream, scream, and after, he's nice like a little lapdog."

Meanwhile, in the video, she's on her knees, things have heated up. With her friend the redhead, they set about giving head to all the guys, one by one. The men approach, they wait their turn, patiently. Pauline tries to count them, but they fill the entire screen and there are still some out of frame. And they suck, and they suck, thighs spread nice and wide so the camera doesn't miss a thing.

Claudine had never fallen in love. Instead, she fell into business: *What are you going to give me to have me?* And no one, ever, hooked her. Except maybe Sébastien. What did she have to gain from that, his coming and doing things, if afterward she didn't even try to use it to hurt her twin? While rummaging through the cupboard, Pauline found little notes scattered around, loads of little lines. About someone she waited for every day but who came only rarely, she would lean out the window and look to see if he was coming. And when he does arrive, he's ashamed, and she can never say to him, "Stay with me, I need you." In one note, she recounts how he asked her if she would really do it, be with him for good. She responded that she didn't know, and he said, "Well, I know. I couldn't be with you. You would screw me over, I'm sure of it," and she decides that he's right.

She and her sister had been face to face, searching for what the other had that she so painfully lacked.

Now it's turned into a marathon performance. Pitiful to watch. She's soaked with sweat and sperm, how many times has she sucked and jerked off and sucked and jerked off? The redhead continues too. They both seem worn out, they try to pretend otherwise, remain all cheerful. They're exhausted, it's obvious, it's odd. And the guys continue to slide in, glide into their mouths, most of them can't even get hard, it doesn't stop them from going.

It continues like that for a while. Pauline fast-forwards until the end. They both end up on the bar, and the guys spray them with champagne. Shower. They cling to each other while waving like queens on parade.

She gets up, looks at the time, she's running late for the meeting. She thinks of everything she has to do before leaving. The right stockings, shoes with heels that aren't daggers, and what is she going to wear today, and how she should have exfoliated but she doesn't have the time, she needs to wash her lackluster hair, and she definitely needs to put on makeup because she has unbelievable dark circles under her eyes. She starts to shuffle around, move heaven and earth to be both presentable and not too late.

It reminded her of Nicolas. It comes back to her these days, desire for him to be there. In front of the video, arousal spreading, she would have liked for him to be there, she would have liked to do it with him.

She sits down again. Where the hell did she put her Bénard pants she was wearing when she arrived, and the shapeless sweater that went with them?

THE BIG BOSS is making a scene, almost as if she'd cheated on him. He asks, "But what are we going to do?"

"It's difficult to deny it."

"So what do you propose?"

"Have to own it."

Martin is almost in mourning too. They broke his doll. The publicist is appalled. "It's really bad for your image, really bad."

"Look around, boys. Everybody does it now, that's what you need to realize."

"You think this is funny?"

A little bit. Now, their idea of the singer, all fresh and vibrant—they can shove it up their asses.

Martin announces, exasperated, "We have to cancel the Élysée."

"Are you crazy?"

"There's no problem, boys: this is kickass publicity."

The big boss is really sulking. She bets that what bothers him most is that he's never seen her like that, like the Claudine in the video; with everything he did to her, he never made her come like that.

THE WOMAN AT the newspaper kiosk next to Nicolas's place knows that he knows Claudine well, so when there's an article about her, she waves him over.

The first few times, it put him in a violent tailspin to see her in the papers. An explosion of missing her. To know, to be able to see, that she still existed somewhere, but that it was happening out of his sight.

Over time, he got used to it, now he reads the papers meticulously. He has fun classifying the photos: Pauline or Claudine? She must have found some of her dead sister and given them to the photographers. He always knows which is which.

Otherwise, it didn't astonish him all that much, that she was on the cover of so many magazines. It had a much greater impact on the newspaper seller, for whom he became a hero within a few weeks because he "knew the singer."

Today, she waves him over with such vigor that he suspects something has happened. She's all shaken up. "For your girlfriend," and hands him a pile of newspapers. He flips through and understands. The video of Claudine. A while back, that had been her latest craze: doing porn. "It opens doors to everything." But after the first film, she had bailed on all the meetings and stopped talking about it.

He had watched it at a friend's house, not even a hint of an erection. That was how sacred their friendship had been.

That's even how he differentiates Pauline from Claudine in the photos: whether he gets hard or not.

The kiosk lady is wholeheartedly on her side.

"How disgusting, bringing out things from the past to harm her. Who knows what she was going through to end up doing that . . ."

But it's clear that she's very disappointed.

"Are you going to the after-party?"

"Yeah, I think I'll stop by."

He had received an invitation to the concert. The first sign from her since that night at Place d'Italie. The concert hall is jam-packed, mainly young girls with piercings everywhere.

Now that the porno is out, Claudine-Pauline is poised to become the muse of all the bad girls. She's handling all the fuss quite well.

When he understood that she was avoiding him, the bubble burst and he dropped back down to earth with a crash. It quickly became unbearable, as soon as he saw a girl, to compare her to Pauline-Claudine and feel the absurdity of a life spent without her.

He was feeling things that he thought only other people felt. That hunger for someone, excluding all the rest.

And his desire to fuck became even worse after having done it. She smells like sex to him.

The light goes out, the typical shrieks in the front rows; it's the intro. A film is projected on the big screen stretched behind the stage. He recognizes Claudine right away, tapping away on the Minitel.

Pauline waits until she's giving head to make her entrance.

She's dressed like the day she arrived in Paris. But she's less timid onstage.

Whistles of approval in the audience, the girls seem to like it.

And then it begins. He's moved hearing her voice, and finds it insufferable to still be so far from her.

"SHE SURE KNOWS how to put on a show, huh?"

"Apparently she takes herself for an artist. She's putting her record label through hell."

"Especially because she doesn't even know how to sing."

"In any case, as long as she doesn't launch her own fashion line . . . Did you see what she was wearing?"

Most of the people at the after-party are talking about things other than the concert. But Nicolas's neighbors are absorbed in their discussion. He's at the bar, he miscalculated his move, is standing where the bartender never comes.

There's a murmur when she arrives—"There she is, there she is"—heads turn, people spread the news. Nobody cares, in fact, but it's still her party and she's on TV sometimes, so they want to see what she actually looks like in person.

She's holding the redhead from the film by the waist, they're both beaming. Visibly wasted, a feverish arrogance.

People surround them, compliments, she smiles at everyone and nods her head, shakes hands.

The big boss bounces around her, makes sure everybody knows: "She's marvelous! Marvelous!"

Finally, Nicolas manages to get a drink. He stands in a corner to down it in peace. He's amused by his own suffering. Has to make an effort not to intervene, push everyone away, and shout, "That woman is mine, there's only the two of us, back off!"

She vanishes from his field of vision, carried away by a sea of morons.

He sets his glass on the bar and heads toward the exit. When he hears her calling his name he's thrilled. She takes him by the arm and follows him into the street. People follow her. "What are you doing?" She signals that she'll be right back.

Face to face, they don't have much to say to each other.

"I thought the concert was really good. More hardcore than grunge. But really good."

"You're wrong. It was really grunge. What's new with you?"

"Still nothing. And you, your new life, it's going well?"

"I'm a storm unto myself, seriously. Did you see that mess around me? I didn't know I liked it, but fuck, I adore it."

"I can tell, yeah."

That douchebag Martin comes looking for her, doesn't even take the time to notice Nicolas.

"Guess who's here, downstairs?"

Overexcited. It must be someone important. Pauline says before leaving, "I'll call you, so we can see each other?"

"If you have nothing better to do, go ahead."

"HI, HELLO, IT'S Claudine. Any chance you're free?"

"Now, even when you call *me* you don't say your real name? Have you totally lost it?"

"No, it's just a habit. Am I interrupting anything?"

"It's fine. I borrowed a console, I was in the middle of killing some Russians."

"I've never played video games."

"I play a little every day."

"Can I come see?"

"Today?"

"Yeah, or whenever you want."

"Well, I'm not super booked. Now works, tomorrow too."

"I've never been to your place. Where is it?"

"Move over, you're taking up all the space."

"Stop making up excuses for why you always lose."

"I don't *always* lose, what are you talking about? I've won plenty of races."

"You won once at the beginning because you got lucky and since then you keep rolling in the grass or driving straight into walls."

"That's bullshit. Let's play again."

He pushes Reset, sits back down. She declares, convinced, "I'm going to destroy you."

End of four races; she came in eighth every time. She says, "I'm sick of this game. It's for little kids. Is there something else we can play together?"

"In James Bond we can chase and shoot at each other."

"Let's see."

She looks outside, it's night. She suggests, "Want to order pizza?"

"With everything you shove up your nose you're still hungry?"

"Yeah. I shove some up my nose every day and I still eat sometimes."

"You've gotten really fucking skinny."

"I eat a little less than before. Actually, sometimes, I'm hungry, but it's impossible to eat. So, let's order a pizza?"

When she arrived, at the beginning of the afternoon, it wasn't very easy at first. Nicolas racked his brains to find a question to ask her or something to tell her. The apartment seemed so small, and the silence so heavy.

Out of desperation, Nicolas had offered, "You want to play?" Out of politeness, and figuring she couldn't take off before at least half an hour had passed, she accepted.

They started a race and forgot to be nervous.

There's something battered about her, a sad side she didn't have before.

He thinks only of lying down on top of her. He wants the heat of her, he wants her to open all her doors to him.

But he feels that it has to come from her. Otherwise, she'll give herself to him just to immediately recoil and it'll start all over again: "I don't want to see you anymore."

That's certainly what she came looking for, but she's afraid of going for it. He has to give her the time to calm down.

He watches her play, tense over her controller. She does what girls do: scolds herself for things nonstop. "Fuck, Pauline, what are you doing," instead of insulting the machine.

He says, "What are you doing? The zombies already ate all your health."

"I'll find some health again, I'm not worried. I don't think you have enough faith in my strategic decisions, you'll see."

"You have to kill the giant, there's plenty of ammo behind you."

"No, I don't kill the giants."

When the sun rises, they go out for coffee. It's clear they

haven't slept, and they giggle nervously over everything. She's excited.

"Those games are great, really great . . . It's too bad we couldn't finish."

"I can save it if you want, I'll wait to finish it with you."

"I have twelve thousand things to do, I won't be back before Christmas—not this coming one, but the one after. So it's better you don't wait for me."

That snaps him back to reality, all at once. Since last night he had forgotten that they didn't see each other every day anymore. He hides it well, but feels hollow inside, he could have suggested *You could just stay at my place* instead of what he asks.

"You're really super busy then?"

"Overbooked, like a fucking yuppie. Yesterday, I was tired of it, I told them I was sick."

"And you're going to record another album?"

"Have to wait a bit, they're still putting out two more singles."

She smiles.

"But I'm in talks for the next one. We're discussing the advance."

"Well if you want me to take care of it for you . . ."

"And you, you still spend your time doing nothing?"

"I also spend some time feeling sorry for myself, but really I don't mind."

She looks at the time, assumes a grave tone, "If I don't leave now I can tell I'm going to waste another day . . . I have to get going."

She takes the receipt, pays, leaves an enormous tip. Since looking at her watch, she has changed slightly, reassumed the attitude of a confident woman.

And she scuttles toward a taxi.

Nicolas goes back home. Smell of old cigarettes. He clears the coffee table, empty cans, coffee cups, box of sugar.

He goes to lie down and sleep. Tomorrow he'll play alone. It's not the same, alone. It's fine, but obviously it's less fun. And there are things you find faster with two.

BEFORE GOING HOME, Pauline stops at the bank to get a new checkbook.

There's a woman in front of her who must be about her age but with three kids. A little girl with a head full of braids who's drawing flowers on a leaflet. She hands it to a man waiting there. Her little brother is terrified, clinging to his mother's leg. The last one she's still carrying, a tiny little baby. She's a very beautiful woman, dressed like she's in North Africa, a red dress with gold embroidery. She waits, the employee verifies something, shakes his head no.

"It hasn't arrived in your account. I'm sorry."

The woman doesn't move. She says nothing. The bank teller repeats, "Come back tomorrow, maybe it'll be here then. I can't do anything for you."

She doesn't make to leave. She stays there, as if she lacks the strength to go back home without a cent, as if she doesn't want to believe it.

Then she calls her little girl, takes her little boy by the hand, leaves, slowly. Her eyes stare straight ahead, big chasms.

The bank teller recognizes Pauline, gives her a big

smile, she says hello, explains what she wants. He asks her, "Would you like one checkbook or two?"

As soon as she's back home, she goes to the answering machine, now a conditioned reflex.

Message from Sébastien, he leaves them now and then. His voice is monotone and sad. "I know the latest with you, all I have to do is turn on my TV . . . but I'd like a real update."

It's that same voice, the one that ripped apart her flesh, made everything turn upside down, shooting blood from her wrists all the way to her skull; now hearing it is just like any other voice, hard to believe that it is, however, the same, it's nothing but another message. All that's left is snippets, a memory of emotion, still a bit of regret, in places. Now completely alone, she isn't mad at anyone.

She never calls him back. She's a little bitter, she'd needed him so badly, during all those transformations, when she felt like she was losing her mind, and it could have been different if he had been there all this time. But above all, she became afraid of him. Of judgment. Not his judgment of her, but the way she would judge herself if she were ever to go back to him. Now that she's alone, she can be the father—egotistical, ambitious, aggressive—and only do what she wants. If she were to be his woman again, she would transform back into a wife, the one who has to help, forgive, be forgotten.

And she really likes what she's become.

It's over, this game of stifling the worst parts of herself. She likes easy money, the kind that comes out of walls, all she has to do is slide her piece of plastic inside. That credit card with the whitened numbers because she uses it to crush powder. She likes to show up somewhere and feel like a magnet, someone under the spotlight. And she doesn't care that people don't like her for who she is, as long as they all pretend.

She even likes the hostility she triggers in people. Gossip is such good publicity, people share whatever dirt they can get on her, and the publicists add an extra dose in transit.

She likes it so much when people insult her that she feels like hatred incarnate. *What's wrong with you, that I piss you off so much? What nasty score do you have to settle with yourself that makes you flip out and look elsewhere, to others?*

She meets people who are all smiles around her; as soon as they get home, they play Claudine's movie, to watch her get fucked.

They can say what they want about her, to her face and among themselves; she has a power over them that exceeds their comprehension. She has done the impossible, it gives her a lot of leverage.

She sits down, listens to an old song, "Do the Right Thing," she would really like to chill and stay in all day. She has a lunch meeting to talk about a commercial.

The big boss says it pays a lot of money. He gets a kick out of her love of money like he got a kick out of how much she liked sex. She still vaguely despises him, and he regularly frustrates her. But she calls him, even without having anything to say to him, he's the one she tells her stories to. He confides in her, too, often mentions money.

It's a bottomless hole, his need for dough. Like a man gorging himself, he's sick from having too much but it's the only way he knows how to assure himself that he's competent: earning more and more and more.

He also talks about his age constantly. She doesn't know what to say to him when he tells her what it's like to be on the decline, how horrifying it is. "Your age is visible in the looks of others, even when you yourself don't think about it anymore. Your skin falls off, your smell changes. It's an unfamiliar body, unlike your own, the one you should have always had, the one you always knew. It's like a pathetic mistake, but there's no one you can complain to. And feeling yourself pass, inexorably, into the camp of old men who until now were on another planet that never concerned you. And on the inside of this body nothing changes, you're the same as twenty years ago, in a machine that's slowly breaking down. And even the suffering of the soul, the disappointments we thought we were used to, with all the time we've had to toughen up. But it's the opposite, they're more damaging than ever. And always feeling them in the same place, it's painful, atrociously painful."

It's precisely because of those moments that she feels the desire to take him in her arms and tell him, *I love your body*, even if it's a lie, because he's right, she remembers it, he has an old man's body. Lie, at least to soften the blow. Like every time she hears about someone else's unfair burden, too heavy for them to carry.

Voice mail. The big boss, as it happens. She picks up immediately, he's worried.

"I called you all day yesterday. You were sick? I almost came by. Is everything okay?"

"Actually, I wasn't even sick, I just really needed some air."

"You could have let me know."

"No, I know you, you would have convinced me to go to all my meetings . . ."

Then she's only half listening. The tiniest thing he has to say takes him thirty sentences to get out. He's loaded with so much stupid shit that he weighs down everything he touches. He says he'll come get her, for the lunch, she says okay and gets ready.

Before leaving, inspiration strikes. She calls Nicolas, wakes him up.

"Sorry, I thought you'd be awake by now."

"I have no reason not to sleep, so I'm taking advantage."

"You told me about a video game store, do you want to meet up later and buy a console together? You give me advice, you help me set it up, that way we can play a little tonight."

"Didn't you have a ton of things to do today?"

"I'm going to cancel. I have a lunch that I'm not skipping but the rest I'm canceling."

"You're right, have to stay grunge."

When she hangs up, she jumps up and down with delight. There's nothing better than getting ready for a super busy day and then bailing.

She won't let the big boss know because he'll throw a fit on the spot.

Nicolas turns the TV around to mess with the wires in the back.

"I have no idea how you installed your TV."

"I didn't do a thing."

"If it was Claudine who did it, that would make more sense."

"You know that you're the only person who talks to me about Claudine without thinking she's me?"

"You're not afraid it'll get out?"

"I am. But it's always the same story: it would be good publicity."

"You transform everything into publicity now?"

"Just watch me."

"And you've never ended up in sketchy situations, people who knew your sister and you didn't recognize them?"

"I have. But since I've become 'somebody,' they think I'm just being pretentious. In fact, I mistake myself for her sometimes. I don't always think about it, that it's all a lie."

"All right, it's working, we can play. Where did you put the games?"

She points to the table, takes a hit off the joint and some still-lit ash falls onto her blouse, she jumps up and wipes at her chest. It makes a little hole.

She asks, "Will you go buy some beer before we start?"

"You haven't changed all that much: you never want to move your ass."

"It's different now. You saw, people recognize me. I can't walk around freely anymore."

"You've found yourself a good excuse."

It's a game with different worlds. There's water. Doors only open with the help of keys that are difficult to find, you have to swim run jump from roof to roof, kill guards, dogs, rats, tarantulas. When the girl finds something interesting she stoops down and says, "Ah-ha." There are disconcerting noises to warn that something bad is about to happen.

They play until late. At the end they find themselves trapped inside an elevator, they have to kill three guys but they have almost no life left and die every time. Pauline is discouraged.

"We should never have saved it here. Now we have to restart the entire thing."

"You're never actually stuck in this game."

"I don't know where you get your ideas from. You can see that it's impossible to kill them!"

"Tonight, because we're exhausted and wasted. But tomorrow, we'll beat it no problem."

"You want to sleep here? We can pull out the sofa."

"Are you leaving super early tomorrow?"

"Don't worry, I won't wake you up. You'll just have to lock the door behind you. That way, before you leave, you can try to beat it."

"Okay."

She points to the sofa. "You know how to open it?" He's still playing, he signals yes.

"I've slept on it before."

She leaves him, she wants him to hold her back, she's relieved he doesn't.

She closes her bedroom door, undresses, lies down. She wants him to enter without knocking and slide between her thighs. She's relieved he doesn't.

In the morning, he's woken up by gunshots and Pauline shouting, "On the first try! Can you believe it?"

"Congratulations. Have to admit you're lucky, that helps."

"Dexterity, agility, strategy, an understanding of the game, impeccable state of mind . . ."

"You're not late?"

"I don't want to go."

"I'm starting to regret bringing you this game."

"I'll finish it, and then I'll get back to a normal life."

"It'll take you a good week to finish."

"That doesn't scare me."

"They didn't say anything about you canceling again?"

"I didn't tell them. They'll figure it out on their own."

"Won't they be worried about you?"

"Yeah. They'll get over it."

THE BOSS WAS sick of calling and Pauline not picking up. He came to her place.

She knows that it's him as soon as she hears the doorbell. She mutes the TV, Nicolas whispers, "Are you expecting someone you don't want to see?"

"It's the big boss. He's so clingy!"

"Go open the door for him."

"I don't want to. I have the right to relax for two minutes, don't I?"

"Yes, exactly, you just have to tell him that."

He insists and rings again. Nicolas also insists, "You have to. What if he calls the police?"

She's afraid, for no real reason. Nicolas's argument persuades her to get up, because it's true that that's what he'll do and it'll look bad, once the door is broken down, the two of them desperately trying to clear a steep incline with fans below that chop Lara up every time she falls through them.

She was right to open the door, the big boss has worked

himself into an indescribable state and at first she thinks that something bad has happened to him. He's pale and trembling, throws himself onto her as soon as he sees her, takes her in his arms, he looks like he's going to sob.

"My precious Claudine, I was so afraid . . . I imagined things, things that were . . . I was so afraid!"

She pats his back. She'd like to go back to playing, but can tell it won't be so simple.

"I'm sorry, I didn't think you'd be so upset. I just decided to switch off for a few days."

Now he's indignant.

"Everyone is looking for you! Don't you realize? That's not professional, Claudine."

It's the worst insult he knows. For him it's very, very bad when someone isn't professional. You can be wretched, dishonest, exploitative, an imposter, just about anything you like, but you must remain professional.

He catches sight of Nicolas in the living room, who had the smart idea to turn off the TV. The big boss thinks he understands everything, without saying hello or anything else, he shouts, "I should have known!"

Turns toward Claudine. "Claudine, get ready, we have a dinner tonight."

Then toward Nicolas. "Sorry, young man, I won't get her back to you until very late."

"No problem, boss. I'm taking off."

She lets him leave, judging that it's the most reasonable thing to do, accompanies him to the door, Nicolas stifles a giggle, then whispers, "You're in for a scolding."

"Tell me about it . . . I'm going to try to get him to play a little, maybe he'll like it. I'll call you tomorrow?"

She closes the door behind him. The big boss is going

around in circles in the living room, still on the verge of tears, he throws up his arms.

"It's all well and good that you have love affairs . . . But that can't impinge upon your commitments. And you know that. What came over you?"

"Don't act like it's the end of the world, I switched off for two days. I needed it. I'm sure the world is still turning. You know me, I'm serious, dedicated, ambitious, it's just a phase, I wanted to decompress."

"Go tell that to the two newspapers you bailed on, and the TV segment you didn't do, and the meeting at the production company that it took me three months to get, you didn't even cancel, the guy was furious, I had to lie to defend you."

"That must have been hard for you, to lie."

She tries to calm him down. He really thinks of himself as her father, someone who knows what's best for her. He asks, "Who was that guy?"

"A friend."

She could explain to him that they're not doing anything together. Because he doesn't say so, but it hurts him, that she shuts herself in with another person. And on top of that, a guy her own age.

And that's what she was planning to do: reassure him. He is, after all, the closest person she has. She is grateful to him for coming to her in person to get her back on track. Enough with the games, she has other things to do.

She opens her mouth to explain to him, *He's just a friend.*

The big boss speaks first. "You sure he's not just a little freeloader?"

"Why do you think that?"

"When someone is in your situation, all the parasites come out of the woodwork, and you know it."

"No, no. He's a good guy."

"Allow me to hold on to my suspicions. In my opinion, a good person is someone who would know how to support you. Not some lazy asshole that lets you cancel all your appointments."

"Allow me to inform you that you can go fuck yourself and that I don't give a damn what you think of him."

The big boss scowls but doesn't get upset.

"You plan on seeing him again?"

"Yes."

"What does he do for a living?"

"Nothing at all."

"But he's not a parasite . . . Come on."

"And you, your wife, she's a parasite too?"

The big boss defuses the situation. He shows her his watch.

"We can't be late. Go get ready, please?"

He looks at her, she's wearing a completely rumpled dress, the first one she found when she got up, her hair's not done and neither is her makeup.

He adds, "It's clear you don't care about making yourself pretty for him."

"He, at least, likes grunge."

"I like you when you're pretty."

That was one of her father's criticisms. Back when she didn't realize that she could look like her sister, that all it took was presentation for a man to find you desirable. She thought that you either had femininity or you didn't; she didn't know it could be manufactured.

She goes to take a shower and get dressed, hears him on the phone in the other room.

They're going to a dinner with *such* fascinating people. She wanted to cancel but the big boss was against it. "They absolutely want to see you. They'll be very offended if you refuse."

Now her job is to honor important people. There will of course be one in the group who will make her feel like an idiot, talentless, like she doesn't merit so much success. There's always at least one. And another to make the comment that it won't last, that she has to take advantage of it, that the public gets bored quickly. Another still to say, kindly, that on top of that, women get old fast.

There will be yet another to tell her a few secrets. Since that porno came out, there's always someone who wants to talk to her about what he's into, with a conspiratorial tone, who just wants to tell her: "You know, I did that with a man," or "I was tied up," or "I'd like to be pegged, but my wife isn't really up for it," or "I like to wear high heels."

There will certainly be several people who will lavishly ignore her, to really make the point that they don't give in to mainstream fads.

And all together they'll discuss, case by case: "What so-and-so does is crap" and someone else "is the only true filmmaker of his generation, what a waste that he's so unknown." It's always the ones no one knows about who are the only legitimate ones. The general public, true boors . . . bad taste, always rewarding the incompetent.

She'll dine with the elite. She won't let out a single giggle. She'll understand nothing of what they say. "You haven't seen that movie?" Poor her, sweet her, ignorant her, fortunately she has a big ass to make up for it, "It's a real gem," and everyone will agree, "Nothing happens in the first hour, absolutely nothing, and out of that nothing surge true moments of grace." There are a lot people who like it that way, that she is as uncultured as she is ravishing. That's their idea of a good lay.

She can't manage to put her makeup on. She screws up one eye, takes it off, screws up the other, starts over.

The big boss has calmed down, he asks her from behind the door, "Almost ready?"

"It'll be another ten minutes."

"Oh, you women!"

What an original comment. She isn't sure what jacket to wear. She says to herself, quietly, "I have such intriguing dilemmas."

Then she does a line and lectures herself. "You won't complain about what happens to you, you won't complain about the life that you lead. Today, the boss upset you, but most of the time you're really happy about how things have turned out for you. And you like all this duplicity. There's only one thing you're in a rush to do, which is to make a second album just to prove to these assholes that you're a big deal and that you sing well. Today, you wanted to stay and have fun with Nicolas, but I know you: tomorrow you won't even think of calling him anymore, he'll feel distant, because it's true, he's a loser, he's not interested in anything, and going out with guys like that always ends up pissing you off."

Doesn't stop her from finding her boss pathetically burdensome, that already-old idiot who acts like a lady, calling it "savoir-vivre."

She's ready to go out. Looks at herself a last time. Smiles at herself in the mirror; she's pretty like that.

She had an idea, just then, while the boss was telling her off. An old idea, utterly stupid.

Tomorrow, she will have forgotten it.

METRO PLATFORM. IT comes by a little less often at night. A banana peel is on the ground. Nicolas skims a poem posted in the station by the RATP. Silence of strangers, the majority have their noses in books. Opposite, an old woman is talking to herself, getting mad at someone who doesn't exist.

The metro arrives, unbearable racket, a catastrophic noise every time.

Pauline didn't call the next day, that didn't surprise him. But she did two days later. "I have so many things to do, I can't meet up, I'm just calling to hear how you're doing."

They talked about a slew of stupid things, she had stopped playing the game. "This week I can't, but right after I'll call you, so we can get to the end."

Then for a month he didn't hear from her again. Not that it really surprised him, or disappointed him, he continued on with his little life.

Yesterday, she called. The drugs were probably really good because she was super bizarre, euphoric, a little too emphatic. He said, "I'll come over tomorrow if you want."

"Perfect."

"So it's safe to say that you're really set on it, finishing this game."

"There are ideas, they come to you, but the next day they're gone. And there are others, they come, and then you can't let them go again. You have no control over it, and sometimes it even surprises you."

"I hear you loud and clear."

"I'll explain better tomorrow, when we see each other."

"Whatever you want . . . And if you're sick of singing, I can tell you're ready for a job coming up with riddles for that game show *Fort Boyard*."

He hopes she's thinking what he's thinking. He hopes she'll open the door and say, "Eat my pussy," and then they'll fuck until it hurts.

A guy has just entered the train, he's tapping on his seat. He's massive, and very unhappy.

The metro stops, Nicolas gets off immediately. He's only two stations away, he decides to continue on foot. Walking beneath the elevated metro tracks, it's cold out, the way he likes.

Rue Poulet, he passes a kid running with the police at his heels. It's pretty rare, after nightfall, for the pigs to still be active in this neighborhood. During the day, he saw it a hundred times from Claudine's window, they wait for there to be four cars and two trucks before they arrest a single person. A crowd gathers around them and there's bellowing, each time it would only take a tiny little thing to turn the situation into a riot, and there are always plenty of people to make some noise. And that has always fascinated him: that the little thing never happens. If just one person were to throw a stone, there would be a riot for an entire week. Four cars two trucks, that's not a lot compared to all these people . . . In plenty of situations, it's the same thing: all that's missing is the first stone.

IT'S REALLY FUCKING clean when he arrives. He's never seen the apartment like this. Claudine didn't like things too tidy, she said it was only the seriously deranged who couldn't handle a bit of disarray. And Pauline had never really dared to disturb anything. Had been happy to maintain the mess.

He whistles, admiring, "You really cleaned up."

"I'm moving out of the apartment, I prefer to leave everything clean behind me. I emptied all the cabinets, I tidied everything."

"You did a good job."

"I've been at it two days."

Talking to him, she puts her finger on her right nostril, then looks at him.

Nicolas asks, "Are you afraid of getting a nosebleed, or what?"

"Yes and no, it's more of a tic . . ."

She sighs, smiles, "Have to say, I overdid it the past two weeks."

"You should be careful. Then again, it's none of my business . . ."

"It's finished tomorrow."

"So, you're moving?"

"I'm leaving. I'm going on a trip."

"Cool! Where to?"

"Dakar."

"That'll be a big change from your neighborhood . . ."

He laughs, mentally stumbles: Why is she taking off, and where did she get the idea to go so far away, without him? He tries to stay in control and keep a semblance of dignity.

"When do you leave?"

"Tomorrow night, but I can change the ticket if I want."

She stares at the TV, switched off, she seems concentrated on something else. It stabs him between the ribs, she can't just run off like that.

He says soberly, "You lied to me then, we can't finish the game between now and tomorrow night."

"That depends. If you come with me, we'll have all the time in the world to finish it."

Bingo. He acts like he doesn't understand so that she really has to spell it out.

"You want me to come to Dakar with you to finish *Tomb Raider*?"

"That, and for a whole bunch of other reasons."

Explosion of joy, he knew it would happen, he acts like a smartass.

"I don't really like foreign countries."

"Where have you been?"

"Nowhere."

"Well that's inconvenient, because I can't stay in France."

He fills their two glasses, messes with her a little.

"Too much success? You're sick of it, you want to be able to walk around in peace without anyone jumping you in the street."

"No, I'm used to that now. I even think it'll piss me off, at first, to go unnoticed."

She thinks about it for a moment. She's acting like the other druggies Nicolas knows, stopping in the middle of an explanation, eyes elsewhere, dropping out of the conversation. Then she adds, "I'll explain what I did, and after, I'll explain what I want to do: a month ago, you know when we saw each other, that day, a little while after you left, I decided that I was bored, and that I was on a slippery slope."

"I thought you were having a blast?"

"Everything was great. Except that there's no end to it. Nicolas, they're all completely depraved. I made myself a list, and I realized: I never laugh. Maybe one or two snickers when someone says something really mean. Otherwise, I never laugh. And you know what that makes someone?"

"Acceptable."

"Super sick, actually, and when you're old it really costs you, to have led the life of a poor loser. Do you get it?"

"Not quite. But I'm listening."

"So for a month I've been shuffling around all over the place, a manic supermodel. I was paid a lot of advances."

"Advances on what?"

"On everything. A new record contract, cha ching, a series of commercials, cha ching again, my memoir as a porno actress, cha ching, and a whole bunch of ridiculous things . . . It was like cha ching cha ching. I put everything in a bunch of accounts, I'm telling you straight: I'm set. And now I can leave."

"You couldn't just go on vacation instead, reflect for a bit? Do all of your ideas have to be so stupid?"

"Listen. I'm all about the advance. As soon as I heard the word, I knew that it was my thing: advance."

"Is it a lot?"

"Combined with what I have from the album . . . Together we can live for ten years doing tons of stupid shit, fifteen if we restrain ourselves a bit. And twenty if we take it easy . . ."

"Together?"

"I want you to come. I didn't really know how to tell you. But I won't go alone."

"That's all really nice, but I'm not a piece of luggage."

"I should have talked to you about it earlier. But I was afraid of changing my mind. At the last minute. That I would want to stay. I was so fucking afraid you'd say no."

He is the happiest of men, it's a thousand times more than he needed to be happy. He masks it all, remains pretty cold. There is still one last little thing he wants to hear her say.

He whistles. "You're getting a bit ahead of yourself. I can't leave just like that . . ."

"I don't understand. Aren't you happy with me?"

"Yeah, sure. But there's a difference between being pretty good with someone and throwing everything away to run off with them . . . And then I'd look like a real asshole, once we're in Dakar, if suddenly you realize that you have better things to do than nothing at all with me, and you ditch me like you did . . . Here, it was fine, I handled it well. But out in the middle of nowhere, that would be harder to laugh off."

"Back then I was young, I knew nothing about life. You are the only person I really get along with."

One by one, the words he's been dreaming of. He plans to take advantage of the situation as much as possible.

"I'm sorry, honestly, I just don't want to. But maybe I'll come visit you, one day . . ."

"Do you want to have sex? Sometimes that makes people fall madly in love and then that'll convince you to come with me."

"To be honest, you're starting to get on my nerves."

He gets up, barely feels his legs. Just a bit of revenge, for what she did to him, and most importantly: make her sweat. Make her wait until the next day.

He turns his head toward her, she's biting her lip until it bleeds, too much coke makes her look crazy. He explains, "That hurts me. It's like you're taking me along in your bags. The way you pull me into your bed to try to make me do what you want. That hurts, I feel like you're just using me."

"I had no idea."

"You've just done too much coke. You've lost the meaning of certain things . . . On top of it, the way you talk to me, you're saying: you're such a loser, you really have nothing going on here, why don't you come and entertain me? Do you understand why that's hurtful?"

"But don't you remember how good it was?"

"Not really, no."

TERRACE OF A big house, right on the edge of the sea.

"Fuck it's nice out."

"Yeah, it hurts your eyes."

The Feminist Press is a nonprofit educational organization founded to amplify feminist voices. FP publishes classic and new writing from around the world, creates cutting-edge programs, and elevates silenced and marginalized voices in order to support personal transformation and social justice for all people.

See our complete list of books at
feministpress.org